The Lady in Pink

Also by J.A. Kazimer

Curses!
A F***ed-Up Fairytale

Froggy Style
A F***ed-Up Fairytale

The Fairyland Murders

Published by Kensington Publishing Corp.

The Lady in Pink

A Deadly After Ever Mystery

J.A. Kazimer

LYRICAL PRESS
Kensington Publishing Corp.
www.kensingtonbooks.com

LYRICAL PRESS BOOKS are published by

Kensington Publishing Corp.
119 West 40th Street
New York, NY 10018

All Kensington titles, imprints, and distributed lines are available at special quantity discounts for bulk purchases for sales promotion, premiums, fund-raising, educational, or institutional use.

Special book excerpts or customized printings can also be created to fit specific needs. For details, write or phone the office of the Kensington Sales Manager: Kensington Publishing Corp., 119 West 40th Street, New York, NY 10018. Attn. Sales Department. Phone: 1-800-221-2647.

Lyrical and the L logo are trademarks of Kensington Publishing Corp.

First Electronic Edition: August 2015
eISBN-13: 978-1-60183-263-4
eISBN-10: 1-60183-263-X

First Print Edition: August 2015
ISBN-13: 978-1-60183-264-1
ISBN-10: 1-60183-264-8

Printed in the United States of America

For John and Jacqueline, better known as Dad and Mom, your enduring love is the very reason both your daughters are still single.

CHAPTER 1

The stench of charred flesh wormed its way into my nostrils, bringing tears to my eyes. Wisps of smoke curled up from the blackened corpse lying on the floor at my feet. Not enough, though, to obscure the taut flesh left on the face. A pair of glasses—thick, black, and round, the kind favored by hipsters as well as the legally blind—was fused to the skull. The poor guy on the floor fell into the latter category. I should know. James Wild, a misnomer to anyone who knew him, was (or rather, used to be) my intern at Reynolds & Davis Securities.

And now he was one hell of an overcooked critter.

Surprisingly enough, given my tendency to "accidently" electrocute my employees, I had nothing to do with James's current extra-crispy consistency. Not that the two cops glaring at me believed a single word of my emphatically delivered plea of innocence.

Detective Goldie Locks, the lead on the case, glanced from James to me and then to my gloved hands. "Mr. Reynolds, do you—"

I cut her off. "Blue."

"Excuse me?"

"Call me Blue." I shot her an innocent smile. "After all, Detective, we're practically family."

Her lips thinned. "How's that?"

"You're a detective." I motioned to the gun on her hip. "And I'm a *licensed* PI. Two peas in a similar pod."

Her snort of laughter filled the room. "Not quite. My partner"—she motioned to the second detective, a man in a boring brown suit named Peter Rabit—"and I are *real* detectives. The kind who protect and serve. You"—her eyes locked on mine—"are a blue-haired menace with power problems and a pink-winged fairy sidekick."

"Half fairy," I mumbled.

"What?"

I rubbed the bluish stubble on my chin, which stood out in direct contrast to the paleness of my skin. I really needed to get out more. Get some sun. Maybe take a nice vacation on some sun-soaked beach. Hell, I couldn't remember the last day it hadn't rained in New Never City. I cleared my throat and repeated my statement, "I said half fairy. Izzy is partially human." Not that my statement mattered. People, especially cops, saw things only in black and white, no shades of pink fairy wings. To them, my business partner, Isabella Davis, would always be one thing—the former freaking Tooth Fairy. A failed one at that.

But I knew better.

Izzy was much more than a nice set of wings, even though she did have a hell of a nice pair. Since we'd reluctantly joined forces a little more than a year ago she had taken my fledgling PI business to unprecedented heights. Reynolds & Davis Securities had raked in more over the last quarter than I'd made my entire career, which, given the state of my career prior to Izzy's and my joining forces, wasn't a whole hell of a lot. But I now had hope for a prosperous future.

Three months ago we'd solved the missing-jewel-encrusted-mittens case, one of the biggest cases of my career. Why some rich asshole had given a pair of mittens encrusted with billions in jewels to his latest mistress was beyond me, but it paid off for our company. The media attention alone made us a household name, even if that household was shaped like a shoe and filled with cheating spouses and embezzling kids no one knew what to do with.

Thanks to that case, we now employed seven full-time investigators, three secretaries, a bitchy receptionist, and James, my recently hired intern whose body was currently smoldering on my apartment floor. Good, still-breathing employees were so hard to find.

How the hell James had ended up fried to a crisp on my shag carpet was a mystery. The last time I'd seen him was yesterday afternoon in my corner office at Reynolds & Davis. He was nagging me about this or that. I never paid much attention to the kid. As I'd said to Izzy a million times, what did I need with an intern? But she'd refused to listen, and now poor James was one large charcoal briquette.

Not that one had a thing to do with the other.

I was fairly sure.

Okay, 80 percent.

My gaze traveled from the corpse to the other side of the room, noting small, barely discernable white clumps of debris along the path. I ran my gloved finger over the closest cluster, studied it, and then drew my finger to my tongue.

I spit the crystallized powder out.

I had a pretty good idea what had happened to James.

And it wasn't good.

CHAPTER 2

"Mr. Reynolds, did you just eat evidence?" Detective Locks frowned, her eyes suspicious and a little confused. She glanced from my finger to the body on the floor, her mouth flattening into a thin line.

I held up my gloved finger, showing her the crusty white stuff before she called the guys in white coats to take my ass away.

"So?" she asked, peering closer at the substance. "You don't wash your floor." She gestured around my less-than-spotless apartment. In my defense, I hated housework, which was why I'd hired a maid. Sadly she'd quit two weeks ago after I'd accidently shocked her for the fourth time. Locks lifted her shoulders in a shrug. "Color me shocked."

I rubbed the crystals between my fingers. Tiny particles drifted to the floor, sparkling in the shaft of sunlight beaming through my half-open curtain. "You're missing the big picture, Detective."

The corner of her mouth lifted, softening her normally beautiful albeit stern features. "Is that so? Why don't you be a good little blue-haired boy and tell me just what I'm supposedly missing?"

I ignored her blue-haired-boy dig and instead focused on the matter at hand. "Murder."

"What?"

I pointed to the white deposits sprinkled across my floor. The trail led from James's charred corpse to a few feet from the body, where a barely discernable size-eleven footprint was preserved in the debris. Locks's gaze followed my finger, her eyes growing wider. "Someone stood right there as this"—I rubbed my fingers together again—"was thrown on the floor."

"And that proves what?" She shook her head. "We already know James Wild was inside your apartment before the accident. He must've dropped his bottle of water on the electrical cord"—she motioned to the twelve-ounce plastic bottle lying on its side—"and it shorted out, electrocuting him in the process. Happens all the time."

"Not quite," I said, stepping over the body to examine the scene closer. There was an electrical cord from a nearby lamp running under the body, the plastic coating slightly frayed. In itself not a huge deal, but add water and a conduit, and anyone standing there for more than a few seconds would turn a nice golden brown.

The white stuff, which turned out to be rock salt, was the smoking gun, though.

For without it James's death looked like an accident—tragic, but nothing more than bad luck for my blackened intern. But rock salt wasn't a common household item, especially in my house. Which meant two things.

The killer had brought the salt with him or her.

And James wasn't the intended victim.

I was.

I smiled at the thought.

Twenty minutes after my big reveal, Detective Locks allowed the coroner to stuff James's charred body into a large, black ziplock baggie and carry it off on a stainless steel stretcher. I watched through dispassionate eyes as the corpse was rolled past, the wheels creaking with each rotation.

The poor guy.

James's only sin was working for me.

And doing a fairly bad job, at that.

Hell, the kid couldn't file worth a damn.

I sighed. If he hadn't let himself inside my apartment, James very well might still be alive. Guilt sparked deep inside me. He'd walked into my murder. I owed it to him to find the killer. Not to mention how much I would enjoy exacting my own revenge. I cracked my knuckles in anticipation. It had been far too long since I'd felt the joy of fist meeting facial bones.

A loud shriek from the hallway drew my attention.

Izzy had arrived in fully pink-winged glory.

"No!" she shouted. I peeked around the doorway in time to watch her charge the gurney where the body bag lay. Her face was as white as snow. And not the kind sold by Mary and her band of little thug lambs. "Blue . . . Oh, God . . . Blue . . ." Big, dripping tears rolled down her cheeks, highlighting the whiteness of her delicate skin. The tears quickly dried, and her expression twisted from grief to rage. Her eyes burned violet with it. "Damn you! I told you to move out of this deathtrap." She followed up her statement with a right punch to the wall a foot from my doorway. Plaster crumbled, leaving a shapely hole in the wall.

"There goes my security deposit," I said, stepping into the hallway to stop her from further assaulting my premises.

Her gaze flew to mine, slowly moving up and down as if checking for bullet holes and bloodstains. Something flickered in her eyes, something I didn't like at all, though I couldn't figure out exactly why. "I . . . I don't understand . . ." she murmured.

A smile lifted the corners of my mouth. "Well, Izzy, it's fairly simple. I'm not dead."

"Then who . . ." She pointed to the gurney and the two terrified attendants standing on each side of James's charbroiled body. Both looked as unhappy as two guys could be while carrying a dead body.

"James," I said.

"James? James who?"

I rolled my eyes. "The intern. The one you hired to torture me. That James."

A wrinkle formed on her forehead, a wrinkle that did nothing to detract from her beauty. "You electrocuted the intern?" Her hands flew to her hips as if she was scolding a naughty child rather than a full-grown man. "Damn it, Blue. Do you know how hard it was to find someone willing to work for you in the first place? I had to *beg* James to take the job."

"I didn't kill him," I said through clenched teeth.

"Oh."

I raised a bluish eyebrow. "Is that all you have to say?"

Her wings fluttered behind her. "Good?"

Again I rolled my eyes. A habit I found myself doing more and more around Izzy. She exasperated me in so many ways, drove me to drink, even more than normal. And yet, I still loved walking into the office and seeing her in all her bossy glory. Apparently I held some latent masochistic tendencies.

I shook my head. Her fairy dust must be giving me a contact high. Why else would I sound like a schoolboy with a crush? I didn't think of Izzy that way. She was like a sister to me. I didn't want her in the slightest way. We were partners. Some might even say friends, if they didn't know anything about our rocky past.

"So what happened?" Izzy's softly delivered question drew me from my thoughts. "How did James end up dead inside your apartment? Was it the wiring again?" The wiring she referred to was the bane of every tenant in the building. The lights often flickered, turning off and on at will during odd times throughout the day and night. About 70 percent of the time the flickering had absolutely nothing to do with yours electrically.

The building was old and inexpensive, which was why I'd first moved in. I'd stayed for a variety of reasons since making it big in the PI business. The biggest of which was, it pissed Izzy off to no end. "Wasn't the wiring"—I paused, weighing my words—"exactly."

Her head tilted to the side, showing off the slender slope of her neck. "What's that supposed to mean? What aren't you telling me, Blue?" Her eyes narrowed on my face. I tried not to squirm. There was so much I wasn't telling Izzy. Things I would never tell her, for both our sakes.

I cleared my throat. "James's death wasn't an accident. He was murdered."

"Murdered?" She shook her head, her mouth a thin line. "Are you crazy? Who would want James . . ." Her voice trailed off as her eyes grew wide. "He wasn't the one they wanted dead." She grabbed a fistful of my shirt, shocking herself in the process as her skin met mine. The small spark didn't seem to faze her. "What the hell did you do now, Blue?"

A good question.

Just one I didn't have a ready answer to.

CHAPTER 3

With Detective Locks's stern warning not to leave the city ringing in my ears, I gave Izzy the slip, ducking out of my apartment while she was down the hall talking to my supposedly psychic neighbor, Gizelle. I headed to the street, lighting a cigarette as dusk slowly shifted to night. A few blocks up I stopped, my gaze scanning the turrets and stained glass covering New Never City's only Catholic church, Our Lady of the Tramp. It had been a very long time since my last confession. I doubted the priest had enough time to hear all of my sins. Hell, I'd committed four of the deadly ones by breakfast. And probably would commit a few more before bed.

That was life in the big city for a PI.

On his day off.

Crushing my cigarette under the heel of my boot, I headed farther up the street. A princess in a tight leather dress called to me, offering more than true love's kiss. Had I not just left the scene of a violent murder, I might've considered taking her up on her offer. That was until I noticed the excess bulge in her tights. "Thanks anyway," I said with a wave.

"Your loss," she said in a deep voice.

Be that as it may, I didn't feel even an ounce of regret as I arrived at my final destination a few blocks up—the Mother Goose. My usual watering hole. What it lacked in atmosphere, cleanliness, and customer service—and it did lack a lot in each—it more than made up for in degenerate clientele and cheap albeit watered-down whiskey. I opened the door, letting the stench of years of smoke, stale beer, and body odor wash over me. For a minute, I felt completely at home.

I was careful to keep my back to the wall as I moved inside. No point being an easy target. If someone wanted me dead he'd damn well have to work for it. I wouldn't succumb to an "accident" like James had, not anytime soon, I hoped. My mind flashed to my intern's burned flesh and I shivered.

My mind drifted to the look in Izzy's eyes when she saw that I was alive earlier this afternoon. I wasn't sure whether it was pleasure, fear, or something much, much worse in her gaze. I shook off that thought. Izzy wasn't the stage-an-accident kind of killer. If she wanted me dead, two things were clear. One, she'd use her hands and/or wings to do it. And two, I'd be dead. No question about it. Izzy wasn't a fairy to be messed with.

So just who wanted me dead?

Another group of winged assholes came to mind. The fairies blamed me for everything, from restarting the bloody hundred-year war with the Shadows to losing their Tooth Fairy. Of course, I held quite a few grudges against the winged devils too. After all, they had tried, desperately at times, to murder me. Not to mention their constant lying, cheating, and shooting off my pinkie toe.

My foot still ached when it rained.

Which it often did in the city.

"Well, well," a gravelly voice called from a ripped barstool a few feet away. "Little Boy Blue. Where you been, sugar?"

Rather than answer, I walked passed the speaker without pausing and flagged the bartender down with a wave. Not one to be ignored, the willowy woman on the stool, her skin yellowed from years of bar smoke and liver disease, slammed her drink on the bar top to gain my attention. "Don't be rude, Blue. Buy a lady a drink."

I licked my lips, slowly turning to face Fern with a raised eyebrow.

She let out a loud snort. "One drink, luv. And I'll make it worth your while."

A shiver of disgust rolled over my flesh. Thankfully I'd yet to get drunk enough to find out if what Fern promised would in fact be worth more than the shots of penicillin I'd need afterward. "I'm good. But thanks anyway."

Her snort was louder this time, echoed by her twin sister, Fern, planted on the barstool next to her. "Not what we heard."

I winced. Had one of my electrified one-night stands been talking out of turn? "And just what have you heard?"

The first Fern sat straighter on her stool, downed the brown liquor in her glass, and smiled with satisfaction. "Many things," she whispered as she waved the bartender over. "A bottle of your finest mead and I'll tell you a story." She paused, licking her thin lips. "About a certain boy with a price on his blue-haired head."

Fern finally had my complete attention. I strode to her stool and leaned down so she could hear my every word. "You better not be playing me." I emphasized my warning by rubbing my hands together, generating glowing blue sparks of electrical current.

Neither Fern seemed overly worried at my threat. Instead both women cackled with humor. "Relax your pretty little head," the closer Fern replied. "We wouldn't want you to strain yourself."

I studied the Ferns, debating. One on hand, the Ferns were known for pulling any scam they could for free booze. Then again, someone had just tried to electrocute me in my own apartment. I pictured James's charred corpse and called to the bartender, "Give them a bottle each. And a whiskey for me. The good stuff." I tossed forty bucks on the bar.

The bartender snatched the money and then slid our drinks across the bar. The Ferns gobbled theirs up as if the liquor might disappear as their youth had. I lifted my own whiskey, swirling it around as I considered what the Ferns might know. Bars were excellent for gleaning information. Get someone a little liquored up and you'd be amazed at what they would admit. Which was why I limited my bar drinking to half a bottle and under.

Once the Ferns finished their drinks, I focused on the one closest to me. "All right. Let's hear it."

She straightened on her stool, her cheeks flushed pink with alcohol-infused delight. "Fern and I, well, we sometimes hear things."

"Uh-huh." I'd used their intel a time or two to solve a case; after all, the Ferns knew every drunk in the city. Men and women willing to sell whatever bit of information they had for another drink. "What did you hear about me?"

Fern frowned, her thin lips all but disappearing in her face. "I'm getting to it, Blue Boy. You're so impatient, always wanting what you shouldn't have. One day someone is going to show you your place."

My eyes narrowed at her commentary, but I stayed quiet. She would get to the point. Eventually. I just hoped I lived long enough to hear it. I let out an annoyed sigh.

She shook her head at the sound. "This is exactly what I'm talking about."

"Can you please get to the point?" I snapped.

Face tight, she finally did what I asked. "Fine. Fern and I were at Pixies the other night when we . . . umm . . . overheard a conversation about you. About a contract on your life."

Considering Pixies Bar & Grill was a Fairyland institution, my question of exactly who wanted me dead was easy enough to figure out. Fucking fairies. Those little demons sure could hold a grudge. "Who was talking?" I think I knew the answer to that question too—Izzy's uncles, Clayton and Peyton. It wouldn't be the first time they'd tried to off me. Then again, I'd thought we'd moved past outright murder after Izzy and I became partners. So much for affected loyalty.

"Two people." She paused, her eyes growing squinty. "Both were hidden in the shadows. So neither of us got a good look."

"Was there anything about the men you can remember? Their voices? Or what they ordered? Anything that can help me?" I growled, thinking about the hundreds of thousands of fairies who lived in Fairyland, not to mention the other seven million nonwinged suspects living in New Never City. "Got anything else to go on?"

Fern shrugged her willowy shoulders. "I think one of them might've been a woman."

"A woman?" Damn, that let Clayton and Peyton off the hook. And I sure had looked forward to exacting a bit of revenge on those two.

"A woman, her hair as blond as spun gold."

My eyes narrowed. "Are you sure it was a blond chick?" Sure I'd had a few bad dates in my time, but not one of them had tried to kill me. Yet. My mind flashed to Bo Peep. Scratch that. Only one had tried to kill me. I was fairly sure it wasn't her, though. Staging an accident wasn't her style. She was much more likely to hire some douche to shank me in an alleyway.

Fern wasn't finished; her brow wrinkled, giving her face an even more scrunched look. "Maybe it wasn't a woman at all. Who can say for sure?"

"You've been a great help." I pulled away from the bar, feeling as if I'd been played. I had my doubts about the Ferns' tale. After all, I was still in the game. I would know if someone had a contract out on me, especially if that someone, man, woman, or fairy, was dumb enough to hold a murderous negotiation in a dive bar.

"You can't have everything," she replied with a snort.

I waved the bartender over again and ordered three more drinks. The Ferns grinned with delight at the prospect of more free booze. I smiled too, but for a far different reason.

The bartender brought my drinks over, and I proceeded to drink each and every one while the Ferns looked on. While it wasn't the most mature payback, it sure as hell made me feel better than I had a few short hours ago when I'd first walked into my apartment and saw my smoldering intern on the floor. I downed the rest of my drink to wash away the image.

CHAPTER 4

A few hours and eight whiskies later, night blanketed the city as I stepped from Pixies Bar & Grill, in the heart of Fairyland, the very place the Ferns claimed to have overheard a blonde talking about my murder. I'd questioned every fairy in sight without luck. Either they weren't aware of the contract on my life or they weren't talking. I suspected the latter. Yet without any leverage, other than threatening to fry a few of them, I couldn't make them talk.

The only saving grace was that the bar served some fairly good whiskey. While the booze had warmed the coldness in my soul, it hadn't quite freed me from the events of the day. James was still very much dead. And it was still very much my own fault.

I swallowed over the lump in my chest as my gaze swiveled up and down the seemingly deserted street. My sixth sense, developed after years of being mugged by ogres and beaten for being blue haired by local members of the Big Bad Wolves gang, screamed danger. Something bad—very bad, in fact—was lurking nearby. I could feel its evil stare, practically smell the stench of its breath.

I reached into the pocket of my jacket, making a show of pulling out a pack of smokes. I lit one, inhaling until my lungs burned with pleasure. If I was about to die, I sure as hell was going to enjoy my last moments. I blew out a steady stream of smoke, using it as a screen to search the shadows with greater focus. There. Up the street just in the mouth of an alley, a flash of something caught my eye.

Was it the same assassin who'd murdered my intern, lying in wait to take me out?

I sure as hell hoped so. It would make the investigation into the murder so much quicker.

Acting for the entire world like a blue-haired guy without a care to his name, I strode slowly up the street, enjoying my cigarette after a long day. With genuine regret I snuffed out my smoke on the oil- and urine-stained sidewalk. Then I reached back into the holster under my armpit. This time I withdrew something, if not much dead- lier, at least quicker to kill. Thanks to Izzy's insistence on my not looking like a thug and scaring off our richer clientele, I carried a .38, which fit nicely in the holster, though it did chafe a bit—one of the perils of responsible gun ownership.

Edging closer to the alleyway, my focus intent on whatever lay ahead, I was shocked to hear a ringing in my ears. I shook my head, trying to stop the noise. When that didn't work I glanced down at my Levi's. Sure enough, my pocket began to vibrate.

I swore softly, lifting the cell phone from my pocket as if it was plague riddled. I hated carrying a cell phone, ever since those damn fairies had bugged my last one. They'd used it to track my every move. If those idiots could do it, anyone could. But Izzy insisted on my carrying the latest smartphone technology, so like a good boy I did as she asked/ordered. "What?" I snapped into the phone after an- swering.

"Is that any way to answer?" Izzy's voice pierced the static. "What if I was a client?"

I grinned at her bossy tone. "I'd wonder what the hell you were doing calling me on my cell phone rather than the office number."

"Blue," she said in warning.

"What do you want, Izzy?" I glanced toward the alleyway. "I'm a little busy, so make it quick."

"What are you up to?" she asked, her every word laced with sus- picion.

My smile widened. "Not a thing. I'm practically a choirboy." Which wasn't far from the truth, but what Izzy didn't know wouldn't hurt me. I straightened to my full six-foot height, my eyes on the mouth of the alley a few short feet away. My focus returned to Izzy. "Are you all right? Did something happen?" I pictured James's charred body and my voice rose an octave. If anything happened to Izzy . . .

"I'm fine," she said. "It's you I'm worried about."

I laughed. "I can take care of myself. You know that."

She snorted, and I rolled my eyes. Damn her. I'd saved her life last year and this is the crap I get? I could damn well take care of myself and anyone else who came along. "Someone tried to kill you today, Blue," she was saying. "If James hadn't walked in instead, who knows what would've happened to you."

As much as I hated to admit it, she was right.

Then again, you only live once.

"Izzy," I lied in my most calming tone, "I'm fine. Really. I'm sure whoever fried James isn't about to try again so soon."

"I'm not going to let you risk your life because you think you're bulletproof." She hesitated for the barest of seconds. "Because you're not."

I made tsking sounds. "If I didn't know better, I'd think that was a threat."

"I'm serious," she said in her sternest voice, which oddly enough turned me on more than I would ever admit. It was like being scolded by a naughty winged librarian. I pictured Izzy's long fiery-red hair wrapped tightly in a bun and thick black-framed glasses slipping down her nose. Not a bad image. "Please don't do anything stupid. Go home, lock the door, and I'll see you at the office in the morning. Together we will figure out who's behind this."

"Izzy, everything's under—"

"Please, Blue," she whispered. "I need you to stay safe."

"Okay," I lied.

"Good," she said, sounding pleased with herself. "I'll see you in the morning, then."

I agreed again, my gaze still fixed on the alleyway. We hung up, and I shoved the cell phone back in my pocket before I bolted toward whatever danger lurked in the darkness ahead.

At the mouth of the alley, I scanned the shadows with my gun. A small squeak echoed off the bricks, and I jumped, nearly blowing a nice round hole in a tiny sunglass-wearing mouse with a cane pin-balling its way through the garbage strewn on the ground.

I frowned, disappointed, as I shoved my gun in its holster. Patience, I reminded myself. Not that it was one of my virtues, if I had any virtues, that is. I had no doubts that whoever had killed James would try to murder me again. I would just have to wait until they made their move. And then I would have them.

I grinned at the thought.

CHAPTER 5

I headed toward my apartment, hoping like hell the charred filet-mignon stench of James had dissipated, not to mention that the cops and crime scene techs had vacated as well. The last thing I wanted to do was sit through another of Detective Goldie Locks's interrogations. She knew as well as I did that I'd had nothing to do with James's murder. Mostly because I wasn't dumb enough to leave my murder victims in my own home.

After all, there were plenty of perfectly good body dumps in the city.

I climbed the steps to my apartment, huffing and puffing from a pack-a-day habit. I asked myself for the hundredth time why I still lived in a four-story walk-up when I could afford much classier digs uptown, a place with an elevator and a doorman so nobody could sneak inside and stage a little mishap. Was it worth it just to ruffle Izzy's wing feathers?

Exhaustion plagued my every step. I needed a solid eight to ten hours of sleep, which had been sadly lacking for me of late. I'd spent too much time working recently to enjoy the finer things in life, like slutty princesses and top-shelf booze. I vowed that as soon as I solved James's murder I would take a nice vacation to some far-off kingdom.

I'd heard Wonderland was pretty rocking as long as you kept your head.

I reached my front door, pausing outside the threshold, thinking about what I'd arrived home to the last time. James hadn't deserved to die. Hell, the poor kid had yet to live. On his days off the only thing he did was play Fairy-Box. I doubted the kid had ever gotten laid.

Not that I was some sort of player. In fact, my last date had ended with third-degree electrical burns and a restraining order. Oddly enough the latter was my idea. Apparently she had a bit of a fetish for electrical current. Two years ago I'd been down for anything, but over the last year I'd matured. I wanted more than a quick zap.

I thought of Izzy and frowned.

Where the hell had that come from?

I wanted her even less than a fried one-night stand.

Annoyed, I shoved my front door wide, expecting a bullet or at the very least another staged accident. When nothing happened I sighed and stepped into the darkened room. It still smelled of roasted pork and hipster, but only a little. I headed for the open window by the fire escape, where a soft breeze ruffled my yellowed curtains. Outside sirens and big bad wolves howled. I lowered the window, leaving it open a crack in hopes of removing the last dregs of smoked James.

"Won't work," a small voice said from behind me.

I spun to face the threat, aggravated to find a two-foot fairy rather than a killer. "What the hell are you doing here, Peyton? Inside my apartment?" It was one of Izzy's self-appointed honorary uncles. I scanned the darkness for his twin brother, Clayton. Thankfully the rest of the room was empty. Odd, since they tended to rove in packs, like wild dogs but with wings, feeding off the carcasses of the damned.

His cherublike face wrinkled, making his chubby cheeks even cuter in the dim light. "After I heard what happened today, I wanted to check in on you. Make sure no one had . . ." He ran his plump finger across his throat like a knife.

I snorted. "Thanks for your concern, but as you can see, I'm still alive, so . . ." When he failed to take the hint and leave, I heaved a sigh. "Was there something else you wanted?"

He sucked in his lips, making wet, slurping noises like a nursing piglet. "Now that you mention it . . ."

I knew it. "No," I said sharply. I wouldn't spit on Izzy's fake uncles if they were on fire. Hell, I was far more likely to actually sizzle them than anything else. That thought brought a genuine smile to my lips.

"If you're not going to help me . . ." He paused as if savoring his next words. "I'll ask Isabella."

"The hell you will." I took a menacing step toward him. Izzy was out of fairy politics. When she'd stepped down as the Tooth Fairy, she'd promised to keep far away from the fairy limelight. No way would I let Peyton drag her back into that vipers' nest. It was far too dangerous. "You did enough to her last year," I said. "I'm not about to let you get in her head again." Seeing as the last time Izzy helped them she ended up as the Tooth Fairy with a target on her back the size of her wingspan.

He inhaled a sharp breath, as if I had offended the little devil. "That's not fair. We would never do anything to hurt Isabella. You know that."

I shrugged. "Not purposely, I suppose. But it doesn't matter, because you will stay far away from her with any of your fairy politics bullshit. Otherwise . . ." I rubbed my hands together, generating flickers of blue sparks. He backed up a step but his chin inched higher, and I knew I'd lost. I blew out a bitter breath. "Fine. What sort of help do you need?"

His cherub cheeks lifted with a grin. "I knew you'd help us. Thank you, Blue. We'll make it worth your while."

I snorted. The last job I did for Clayton and Peyton nearly cost me my life, and the tiny demons had yet to pay me a dime. In fact, they'd written me a check that bounced. Twice. Not that I needed their money. Not anymore, thanks to Izzy's business acumen. But I did want something from him. Something only he could give. "If"—I emphasized the word—"I help you, you have to promise to leave Izzy out of it. No playing both sides." Fairies, the twins in particular, were known for double-crossing anyone. They would smile sweetly and then stab you in the back with a sharpened toothbrush without batting an eyelid. It was one of the things I liked best about the sawed-off demons. Just not where Izzy was concerned. She foolishly trusted the twins, and I'd be damned if I'd let them betray her.

Peyton tried his best to look outraged by my statement but failed. Instead he reluctantly agreed. "Okay. Isabella won't hear a word about the missing fairies from me or Clayton. I promise." He held up his hands to show that his fingers weren't crossed. When I motioned to his toes, he kicked off his shoes to prove he'd left them uncrossed as well. "Happy now?" he asked with a sneer.

I nodded, though "happy" wasn't quite the word I would use for finding myself a pawn in their fairy scheme. "So what's this about missing fairies?"

"Over the last few months nearly a hundred fairies have gone missing," he whispered. "No one thought much about it since they were fringe fairies." A fringe fairy was one who lived outside the protection of the Fairy Council. They usually lived in small bands, scavengers searching for non–Tooth-Fairy–acquired dentin. Without dentin no fairy could survive for long. A week, tops. Which was why the Tooth Fairy existed, to collect teeth for the council. "Then a few fairies from the outskirts of Fairyland began to vanish too," he said. "And we knew something was very wrong."

"No one knows what happened to them?"

"One day they were there, and the next . . ." He shrugged his tiny shoulders. "I fear the worst."

I suspected he wasn't far off. Fairies just didn't up and disappear. Someone—or worse, something—had snatched them. "Why would someone want a bunch of fairies?" I asked, not expecting an answer. The only enemies they had that I could think of, other than me, were the Shadows, and they'd been underground since last year. More important, I doubted the Shadows would want to keep a hundred fairies locked up for months. They were much more likely to kill the fairies outright, leaving tiny corpses in their wake.

Peyton scratched the grey whiskers on his chin. "I can think of a number of reasons. After all, we make fine houseguests . . ."

I rolled my eyes, which oddly enough gave me a better reason, this one much more realistic. "Dust," I said, snapping my fingers. A small bolt of electricity shot out, leaving a smoldering patch of carpet on the floor. I stomped it out with the heel of my boot. "Someone is taking fairies for their dust."

Peyton's eyes widened. "Oh, this is bad. Very bad."

I nodded. An average fairy, as long as he or she ingested enough dentin, would produce about a pound of fairy dust every night. The fairy would then spend much of the morning shaking it off, ridding his or her body of the stuff in order to function throughout the day. Dust often acted as an evolutionary deterrent for any and all predators, sort of like the horrible taste of a brightly colored butterfly. If attacked, a fairy would shake his or her wings, flinging dust at the predator. Since dust acted on the nervous system, as little as half an ounce would incapacitate an attacker for hours in a relaxed, pain-free, and numb state.

Any more of the stuff and you'd be in the morgue.

Having been on the receiving end of the dusty stuff more times than I cared for, I could attest to the intense aftereffects. It was also highly addictive, hence the common use of dust on the streets. Over the last few years the increase in dust addiction had blossomed into a full-on epidemic in the city. No longer were the addicts content to stuff it up their noses; they'd begun to shoot it straight into their veins.

If some drug kingpin was kidnapping fairies for their dust, things would only get worse on the streets. I closed my eyes, picturing the chaos already filling the city, from Zen-spouting trolls to flesh-eating ogres, and everything in between.

One of the many reasons I loved living here.

But I drew the line at drugs.

At least the hard ones.

Dealers preyed on the innocent, turning kids into addicts with a single hit, forcing young girls and women alike to sell their bodies and souls for a few bucks. Not that I wasn't all for the free market when it came to sex. But I preferred willing partners with plain old greed in their eyes rather than track marks on their arms.

"Okay," I said to Peyton. "I'll look into it. But you have to keep your mouth shut. One wrong word and whoever is keeping the fairies might decide to cut his losses and kill them all."

His hand flew to his puffy lips. "I won't say a word."

My gaze narrowed on his face. "Not even to Clayton."

"But—"

I shook my head. "Your brother's got enough to worry about with the upcoming election. He doesn't need this hanging over his head too." With Izzy's encouragement Clayton had tossed his hat into the ring for the first official democratic election for Tooth Fairy. Now, with less than a month until Election Day, neither twin had much time to do anything but kiss winged babies and fairy butt.

"You're right," he said. "We need to focus on what's important."

My bluish eyebrow rose.

Peyton had the grace to blush. "I meant, we should focus on the election because you are going to focus on the more important matter of finding the missing fairies."

"Uh-huh."

He nodded once. "Now that that's settled, I'll leave you to your dinner."

"Dinner?"

Frowning, he motioned to my kitchen. "Aren't you barbecuing?"

Rather than answer, I walked him to the door, promised to call as soon as I learned anything about the missing fairies, and shut the door in his face, which wasn't nearly as satisfying as I'd hoped.

With a sigh I went in search of a can of air freshener.

CHAPTER 6

The next morning as the sun broke through the cracks in my bedroom window I yawned and stretched. Little bluebirds chirped outside, mocking me. I hated mornings. All mornings. But especially this one. Izzy had called me again last night, sweetly requesting my presence at the office by eight A.M.

I glanced at the clock by my bedside.

Nine fifteen.

Oops.

In my defense, I'd been a wee bit drunk by the time Izzy had called last night.

I would've agreed to anything.

Unfortunately, all she wanted was for me to meet with the new VP of marketing she'd recently hired. I dreaded it, but it was part of the job. Or so Izzy told me time and again. "You need to make more of an effort with our employees," she often said. "Get to know them. Let them get to know you instead of walking around the office glaring at everybody."

That was why I now found myself slowly getting out of bed, mostly because of my advancing age, and heading for the shower. Thirty-one was a bitch. Everything ached, from my littlest piggy to the ends of my hair. Naked, my pale, flesh-toned skin nearly blinding in the sunlight, I padded across my bedroom to the bathroom. I avoided glancing in the mirror, knowing just what I would see—red-rimmed eyes, a bluish five-o'clock shadow, and a head full of hair badly in need of a cut. My hair stood on end from both static and my own electricity, not to mention a slight beer gut, which stood out on its own as well, a new addition to my already vast array of physical shortcomings.

With a wet smoker's cough I vowed to take better care of myself.

Like I did every morning after hacking up a smoke-infested lung.

Stepping into the shower, I cranked the water to hot and enjoyed a rainbow of blue sparks flickering off my body as I washed myself clean. After scrubbing my parts twice, I turned off the water and toweled dry. Still taking my time, mostly just to annoy Izzy, I slowly pulled on a clean undershirt, a silk dress shirt, a freshly pressed pair of suit pants, and shiny loafers. As much as I hated the dress code of corporate securities, I had to admit I looked damn good in it.

However, I absolutely refused to wear a tie.

Any tool who did was asking for trouble.

It took only a few seconds when in a fight for your life to twist your opponent's tie into a garrote, thereby ending the fight with little muss or fuss. Never would I give someone that kind of leverage.

Besides the snub-nosed .38, the final accessory to my attire was a pair of black leather gloves. No use electrocuting the clients before they paid their bills. Fully dressed, I headed to the kitchen for the breakfast of champions: leftover coffee from the day before and a stale roll with what looked like flakes of basil in it but turned out to be green mold. I spit the roll out, promised my stomach a big lunch, and headed off to work.

I wasn't whistling.

Far from it, in fact.

I grabbed the Fey Train uptown to the office of Reynolds & Davis Securities. The building that housed our offices dwarfed the surrounding buildings by ten stories at least. Like a beanstalk, the building rose into the clouds, disappearing into the sky. When we first partnered up, Izzy had insisted on new digs, saying my old office was too small for a growing business. Which it was, but given our financial standing, it was hard to rent anything bigger inside the city limits, and I'd be damned if I'd commute to the outer kingdoms. A two-hour drive to go twenty miles held little appeal. But I suspected Izzy's insistence on moving had more to do with my nearly dying inside my old office than a longing for more expensive digs. I never put the question to her, though. Instead, I agreed to look at a few places within our price range, which was about a thousand bucks a month at the time. A stretch, but anything under a grand meant we'd be doing business out of a box under a bridge in Troll Town. Not a pleasant thought.

Two days after that, Izzy dragged me to what were now our offices, way up on the fortieth floor of a mass office complex. Lawyers, stockbrokers, and other assorted corporate riffraff worked on the floors above and below us.

We actually prettied the place up a bit.

Or so Izzy claimed was the reason the rent was so cheap. I hadn't believed her at the time, and I still didn't. My only hope was that the twins weren't our landlords. I'd had enough of their interfering innkeeping at my old place.

Shaking off the memory, I took the elevator to the fortieth floor, inanely singing along to the Muzak version of "Ring Around the Rosie" blasting through the elevator speakers. To tell the truth, I was as pleased as the rest of the riders when the doors opened at the brightly lit offices of Reynolds & Davis.

A sleek receptionist with long flaxen curls, a color not found in nature, who may or may not have been a former princess and contestant on *The Bachelor: Prince Charming Edition*, smiled in welcome. Until she saw it was me, and then her smile slipped a few degrees south. "Mr. Reynolds, how nice to see you," she lied without a hint of sincerity.

"Right back at you," I said to her as I pulled off my gloves. I would've used her name but I couldn't remember it to save my life. I did, however, remember shocking her about a month ago. Not entirely my fault since she'd been the one to grab my ass at the after-work office party. My eyes narrowed as I considered the color of her hair, thinking of the Ferns' description of the woman with hair the color of spun gold. I quickly shook off my growing paranoia. "Is Ms. Davis in?" I motioned to Izzy's office, which sat at the opposite side of the office from mine.

The receptionist glared at me. "I'll check." She pressed her long, manicured nail against the intercom and then spoke quietly to whoever answered. She seemed to take great pleasure in making me wait for an answer. Seconds turned into minutes. Finally her eyes met mine. "Ms. Davis is in a meeting at the moment. She will be with you shortly."

I laughed and headed toward Izzy's office, the woman's screeches following me down the hallway. I didn't bother to knock on Izzy's door; instead, I pushed it wide open. "Honey, I'm home."

Izzy rose from her chair, looking gorgeous as always. Her long red hair curled around her shoulders, brushing her ample breasts, which were hidden inside a charcoal business suit. The only hint of color besides her hair was a bright red camisole barely discernable underneath her form-fitting jacket. Her indigo eyes flared almost purple with anger. But her lips twisted into an indulgent smile. A smile she used too often when in my company. "Blue," she said, her voice husky and soft. "I'm glad you're here."

I raised an eyebrow.

"You're just in time to meet Clark Boyer, the third . . ." Her eyes narrowed when I failed to respond. "Our new VP of marketing."

I nodded to the guy seated in front of Izzy's desk. He rose, a good four inches taller and twenty pounds of pure muscle heavier than me. He wore a Grimm Brothers suit that probably cost more than my rent, and his hair was slicked back with too much pomade.

I squinted at his do, fairly sure he dyed his hair. That shade of black wasn't found in nature. And was that a widow's peak peeking from his forehead? Suddenly I felt a lot better about Clark. Until I noticed how Izzy was looking at him, and he at her. My throat grew dry and my palms started to sweat. Not a good thing when you're electrically challenged.

I cleared my throat, trying to dispel the sudden rush of current inside me. "Pleased to have you aboard." When the hell did I start sounding like a boat captain? I shook off that thought, stepping forward to shake Clark's hand.

"Don't," Izzy ordered, her eyes darting to my outstretched hand.

Clark froze, his hand a few inches from mine.

I winced, pulling my electrically charged hand back. "Oops. Better not."

A warm smile split Clark's too-handsome-to-be-good-in-bed features. "That's right. Izzy told me about your . . ."

"My what?" My jaw clenched as I looked from Clark to Izzy. "Izzy," I said in a sarcastic voice, "just what secrets have you been sharing?"

"Behave," she hissed in warning. She turned to smile at Clark. "Clark's first priority is increasing our brand. He wants us to have a greater presence on all the social media sites, especially Fairybook."

Brand? Since when did a PI need a brand? We followed cheating husbands and white-collar crooks. What else was there to say? I kept my opinion to myself, though, at least for now. But I vowed to talk some sense into Izzy as soon as we were alone. She might be a whiz when it came to making money, but I knew what our clients wanted, and it sure as hell wasn't a Fairybook presence. "Okay, then," I said flatly. "Izzy, when you're done here, I'd like to talk to you about a couple of things . . ."

She nodded. "I'll come to your office."

"Thanks." I turned to Clark again. "Nice to meet you."

"You too," he answered. "Very much so."

At his words, a vague sense of uneasiness filled me. I nodded once and then walked out of Izzy's office. I could feel Clark's eyes on me, watching, assessing. I didn't like the feeling one little bit. Something was up with that guy. I wasn't sure what, but I suspected it had something to do with his interest in my partner.

The thought of them together left me cold.

Odd when one burned just above a hundred degrees.

CHAPTER 7

I walked down the long corridor to my office, my footfalls swallowed up by the thick carpeting, with the exception of the sharp crackle of static electricity building around me. Outside my office door, I pulled to a stop. The shiny nameplate on my door brought a smile to my lips—"Blue Reynolds, CEO."

Not that the title mattered. I could say I was a CEO all I wanted, but when the chips were down, Reynolds & Davis was Izzy's baby. I appreciated her attempt at including me in the daily operations, but I was and always would be a PI, a private dick, ready and willing to kick ass and take names in order to solve a case, not some corporate stuffed shirt. Not that there was much ass kicking to do. Investigating in this day and age was all about computers, the Internet, and electronic clouds filled with everything a PI needed to know.

I missed the old days.

But I wasn't a true Luddite. I used computers and other electronic gadgetry when the investigation called for it, which seemed like more and more often.

I sat down in my high-backed office chair, running my hand over the desktop, feeling as worn as the wood under my fingers. The desk was the only piece of furniture from my old office. Each pit, scar, and fingerprint scorch mark told a story I'd explained when Izzy first protested my choice in furnishings. I'd pointed to a gouge mark on the side where I'd smashed a gnome's head into the wood when he failed to pay for an array of photographic evidence that his lovely bride-to-be had quite the billy-goat fetish.

In the end Izzy had agreed to keep the desk, but everything else in my office, including the half-empty bottle of year-old scotch, had gone straight to the Dumpster. Though I missed my old office at times, missed the smell of mold and case files, I had to admit my new office wasn't too shabby. For one thing, it was three times the size, smelled like a new car, and lacked the general chaos and clutter of the old office. When I needed a file now, I pressed the intercom buzzer and some lowly file clerk set it on my desk a few minutes later. Sort of like an investigational drive-through.

To my surprise, when I opened the laptop computer on my desktop it flickered to life. Odd, since I could have sworn I'd shut it down the day before so it could do some random updates or whatever it was computers did when their users weren't around. I suspected it was something to do with plotting to take over the world.

A file folder sat open on the screen, displaying it for the world to see. Not that the world cared one way or another about my quest to find a former nurse at the New Never City Hospital named Christine Connors. Only I cared about her, since she very well might hold the key to finding out my true identity and ending my electrified curse.

Not that I'd had a single break in my search for the elusive Ms. Connors. The file I kept locked in my bottom desk drawer, a file only three people knew of—well, two now that James was dead—was only about an inch thick, but it held years' and years' worth of my life. Years I'd spent searching for the truth behind my birth and the subsequent electric curse. I often asked myself why my parents had abandoned me on the steps of an orphanage. Was it because of my electrical curse? Was said curse genetic? Or more of a freak mutation? But even more important, was there a way to end it? Would I ever be free?

I shook off my wayward thoughts, closed the computer file, and got down to business. Fairy business. I did a quick search on all the interwebs for any mention of the disappearing fairies. Finding nothing, I moved on to my less straightforward investigational methods. I contacted my informants in the underworlds, both figurative and literal, offering a reward for any information pertaining to the missing fairies or my attempted murder.

As I was making my last call, a knock sounded on my half-open office door. "Come in," I called, but no one entered. At least as far as I could tell. Then a small, high-pitched voice reached my ears and I glanced over the edge of my desk to see a green-winged fairy named Jonas. I sighed, annoyed by the never-ending assortment of winged demons in my life. If it wasn't for Izzy I would've wiped my hands clean of the lot of them or, better yet, electrocuted the entire batch as a public service.

"What do you want, Jonas?" I asked, ending my call with a less-than-noble prince with ties to every villain in the surrounding countryside.

Jonas crawled into the chair in front of my desk, his cherub face as innocent and clear as a baby's. I didn't buy it for a second. Fairies were far from innocent, this one in particular. I repeated my question in a tone destined for an answer.

"I don't want anything, Blue," he said. "I have something for you."

I snorted.

"No. Really."

"Okay." I rubbed my hands together in warning of what would happen if Jonas was playing games. "I'll bite. What is it you have for me?"

"Information."

My eyebrow rose. "Is that so?"

He nodded. "I . . . kind of figure I owe you . . . for giving me a job after the council fired me . . ."

Considering it was Izzy who'd forced me to employ Jonas as a nighttime office security guard after the Fairy Council had canned his ass following his role in last year's toothy folly, his gratitude was a bit misplaced, but I wasn't one to let a little thing like the truth muddy up the waters. "So what sort of information do you have?" I asked.

He licked his lips. "Two nights ago, while I was on duty, one of the alarms went off."

Now he'd caught my interest. I leaned forward. My chair creaked in response. "Did you check it out?"

"Yes." He nodded vigorously. "It turned out to be nothing, really. Just someone working late. But when I was looking around I noticed something else."

I rolled my eyes. Jonas was not one for making a long story short. "What?" I snapped when I couldn't stand his rambling anymore. He jumped in the chair, which made me instantly sorry for the chair, as a burst of fairy dust rained down from Jonas's wings. Guess he hadn't had his morning dust off just yet. I inhaled the barest of whiffs of dust, just enough to take the edge off our continued conversation.

Jonas glared at me but continued his tale, brushing off the dust on his sleeves. "A light was on in your office. I checked around, but nobody was inside. Since only you and Isabella have a key . . ."

Damn her. Izzy had no business sneaking around my office, let alone sneaking around late at night. We were partners. If she wanted to know something, she should've asked. Not that I would've necessarily shared whatever information she wanted with her, but it was the thought that counted. Another thought occurred to me at the mention of Izzy and keys. Since she was the only other person with a key to my apartment too, how had James gotten inside? Had he stolen her key or mine? If so, why? I needed to find out why James was at my apartment in the first place. I decided my best course of action was to search James's cubicle.

"Sorry I couldn't be of more help," he said, drawing me back to the conversation at hand.

"Yeah," I said waving him off, my mind still focused on James's death. "Thanks."

He nodded, hefting his small body from the chair and heading for the door. "Blue," he said, stopping in the doorway, "I hear you might have an opening for a new intern . . ."

CHAPTER 8

Around three in the afternoon, just as my eyes had begun to cross from hours behind the computer, another knock sounded at my open door. I glanced up, smiling when Izzy appeared in the doorway looking as fresh as a morning glory at first light, while I felt much like the stuff used to fertilize said flower. I'd spent most of my afternoon searching James's cubicle, which sadly turned up nothing of interest. The kid didn't even keep a calendar, let alone a list of possible murder suspects. The most I found was a matchbook from a Fairyland strip club, Wings, known for its fruity drinks, winged pole dancers, and short, seedy clientele. The kind of place one could order chicken wings and a hit man for less than I paid in taxes. James didn't seem like the chicken-wing or short-hooker type, so I had to wonder why he'd ventured to the strip club in the first place.

"Maybe you should take a vacation," Izzy began, rubbing her fingers against her neck, a sure sign she wasn't comfortable with the conversation. "Go someplace fun. A beach."

I snorted, half rising from my office chair. "This coming from the same woman who complains when I'm in the office less than fifty hours a week." I rubbed my chin, raising my bluish five-o'clock shadow with static electricity. "I can't help but wonder, are you trying to get rid of me?"

"Of course not," she said. "I just think you'd be safer out of town."

"Worried about me?" I grinned. "How sweet. I didn't know you cared."

Rather than respond with a smart-mouthed comment as I expected, she said, "I wouldn't know what to do if something happened to you."

"Is that so?"

"I wouldn't know what to do with the company." A small smile graced her face. "The investigation part is your baby."

"Right," I said. "Reynolds & Davis comes first." To her it always would. A part of me welcomed her cold-blooded business sense. Too much was at stake to mess it up with emotional declarations.

"So about your trip . . ."

I shook my head. "I'm not leaving, Izzy."

"But—"

"Let it go," I ordered.

Her hands flew to her hips and her eyes turned violet. A sure sign I was in for a fight. I steeled myself for the onslaught. It wasn't long in coming. "Do you have any idea how dangerous it is for you to be here?"

I winced, picturing James's burned corpse. His death was my fault. No matter how much I denied it. He died because of me. Maybe she was right. If I left, no one else would get hurt. Including her.

"I didn't mean—"

I waved her off. "I know."

"James was a sweet guy," she said, wrapping her arms over her chest as if to ward off whatever evil had befallen him. "A good worker too."

I shrugged, a rush of guilt sparking along my nerves. I should've paid more attention to him, thanked him more often, or, at the very least, kept him out of harm's way.

"He idolized you," Izzy was saying. "Wanted to become a hard-broiled PI one day."

I ignored the "broiled" part of her comment and asked instead, "Do you have any idea why he was at my apartment?"

"Yes."

My forehead wrinkled. "And?"

"It was my fault."

"I don't understand."

"It was my fault." Her face crumpled under the weight of her words. "I killed James."

CHAPTER 9

Under normal circumstances, Izzy wasn't prone to dramatics like her fairy brethren. But no sooner had she admitted to killing James than she spun on her high heels and dashed from my office, her face in her hands. I ran after her, but I was too late.

She'd already barreled straight into the path of our new VP of marketing. He caught her with one hand before she hit the ground. My dislike of him intensified as his hand slid up the small of her back. "Are you all right?" he asked her, glaring over the top of her head at me. I raised a blue eyebrow. He seemed to remember his place, for he quit glaring and refocused his attention on the half fairy in his arms.

She wiped her eyes with the back of her hand. "I'm so sorry. Please don't get the wrong impression of our company. For the most part, we don't condone nervous breakdowns."

I reached for Izzy's shoulder but dropped my hand before I made contact. The last thing I wanted to do was hurt her. I looked up at Clark. "But we do offer full medical"—my lips curved into an affected smile—"so don't be afraid to try BASE jumping. Now, if you'll excuse Ms. Davis and me, we have an important matter to discuss."

"Of course," Clark said, holding Izzy a few moments too long before finally releasing her. "If you need me . . ." He motioned to his office, next to Izzy's. While his office was smaller than mine, it was closer to Izzy, which bugged me for reasons I didn't want to explore too deeply.

I smiled tightly. "I doubt we'll need your social media expertise for this one, but thanks anyway." I motioned Izzy forward. "After you, Isabella."

She glanced at me through veiled lashes, nodded once, and slowly walked to her office, her head held high. I followed, wondering what the hell was going on.

As soon as I entered Izzy's office my questions flew from my mind. Or most of them, at least, with the exception of who the two three-foot guys with red wings wearing ninja outfits and standing on each side of her desk were. Izzy stood in front of her desk, her face pale in the fluorescent light. She looked far more beautiful than a confessed murderess should.

"What's all this about you being responsible for James's death?" I asked her, ignoring the two red-winged interlopers. I wanted to get to the truth as quickly as possible, sort of like ripping a Band-Aid from a fresh wound. Not that I believed for a second that Izzy had actually killed James. But something was going on in her devious mind. That something didn't bode well for me or anyone else.

She took a shuddering breath. "I asked him to do me a favor."

"What?"

"I knew you'd forget, so I asked James to pick up your tuxedo from the dry cleaners and then bring it to your apartment." She paused, her bottom lip trembling. "I gave him my spare key."

I closed my eyes, remembering the burned piece of black tie clutched in James's locked fist. "Clayton's fund-raiser."

"It's tomorrow night." She sniffed once. "I didn't . . . I would've never . . ."

A hot burst of anger filled me. "Stop it," I said in a tight voice. "This wasn't your fault."

"But if I—"

"No," I said, quickly filling her in on what the Ferns had claimed to see, a woman with hair as blond as spun gold discussing my murder. "Since you don't have that color hair, let alone drink in places like that, you are not responsible. Get it?"

Her eyes met mine. "You have to promise me something."

"I'm not running from this." I cracked my knuckles, causing sparks to burst from my fingertips. "I will find whoever did this . . ."

"Good."

I smiled, glad to have her support. For once.

"Just one more thing . . ."

Shit. I waited for the other glass slipper to drop. It wasn't long in coming. "I'd like you to meet Right and Left," she said, motioning to the fairies on either side of her. They were dressed in the typical black *keikogis* worn by the Fairy Council's elite forces, which were known as the Tooth Unit, warriors in the fight against oppression and tooth decay. "To protect and floss" was their motto. Unappealing for sure, but they worked hard at guarding the Tooth Fairy.

I was pretty sure I could take both of them without breaking a sweat. I began to say as much, but Izzy's glare shut me up. "Since you won't remove yourself from danger, I've hired Right"—she pointed to the fairy on her left—"and Left"—this time she motioned to the toothy ninja on her right—"to watch your back."

"No."

She laughed without an ounce of humor. "You have no choice."

That's where Izzy and I disagreed.

Blue Reynolds always had a choice.

I just usually picked the wrong one.

But not this time.

I shot Izzy my most sincere of smiles, one guaranteed to ease even the purest of princesses from her chastity belt. "Whatever you say, sweetheart." I paused, my gaze hot on hers. "You're the boss."

CHAPTER 10

A few minutes later I was standing on the street outside our office building, Right and Left standing a few feet behind me. Since I was a great detective I quickly realized the obvious; Izzy had wanted me out of the office. I knew this because she said, "Have a nice night." Then she proceeded to walk me out of her office, slamming the door behind me.

Like I said, I'm a hell of a detective.

I looked at Right and then Left, debating. I could give them the slip now, but what was the point? If Izzy wanted to waste her dough by hiring these clowns, I'd play along. For now. It wasn't like it would be too hard to ditch them; after all, their legs were fewer than ten inches long. Not like they could run after me.

I smiled at the image and then reached into the pocket of my jacket to pull out a pack of cigarettes. I lit one up, blowing out a stream of blue smoke in a small act of rebellion. While I was enjoying the toxic burn of smoke entering my lungs, my cell phone rang. For a second I wondered if Izzy had slipped some sort of smoke detector into my clothes. Not completely out of the realm of possibility, since she had bugged my phone on more than one occasion. To say we had trust issues was an understatement.

When my phone continued to ring I pulled it from my pocket and checked the caller ID. "Unknown number" flashed across the screen. I'd learned long ago nothing good came from an anonymous number. Or anonymous sex, for that matter, unless one liked telemarketers and STDs.

"Reynolds," I answered reluctantly.

Static crackled, and then a mere whisper of a voice drifted through the line. "Drop your investigation."

"What?" I said, cupping the phone tighter. The stench of burning smartphone tickled my nostrils, so I reluctantly eased up my grip.

"Stop investigating now or else."

"Who is this?"

The line went dead.

I stared at the unknown number flashing on my screen and then slowly put the phone back in my pocket. I smiled, for the first time all day feeling as if I was finally making progress. On what, I had no idea. The caller should've been much more explicit about what I was supposed to stop investigating. After all, I was currently juggling ten open cases, not to mention James's murder, Peyton's missing-fairies case, and the mystery surrounding my own birth.

My stomach growled, reminding me that I'd forgotten my promise of a large lunch and it was now closing in on late-night-snack territory. I flagged down a passing taxi, and the three of us got inside, Right and Left flanking me.

As we drove through the city, darkness claimed the night and a chill settled in the air. The moon hung a mere sliver in the sky. As we drew closer to my apartment, I shivered in my suit jacket; not from the cold, but like someone had just walked across my grave. Most people went happily ever after without ever seeing a corpse outside a funeral parlor. I wasn't that lucky.

My job all but guaranteed I'd see things others wouldn't.

Maybe it was time to reevaluate my life goals.

Of which I had two at the moment.

The incredibly large lunch I'd promised my stomach about twelve hours ago.

And a very big glass of whiskey.

No ice. Not only did ice water down a perfectly good buzz, but the damn things always brushed against the metal filling in my right back molar, shocking the shit out of me.

I took a deep breath of semi-exhaust-filled air as we exited the cab, feeling the energy pulsing through the city. It was as if the city knew something the rest of us didn't. Was it a warning or the rush of Fey Trains beneath my feet?

I motioned to the darkened street that led to my apartment. "I'll be fine from here," I said to my winged stalkers/molar guards. Apparently they didn't get the hint. Right flanked my left, and Left did the same on my right. I rolled my eyes but didn't press the issue. It was

late, and I was too tired to deal with fairy dramatics. After a nice dinner of pudding, pickled peppers, and pie, I'd toss the short bodyguards out.

My mouth watered just thinking about the next hour, which said
something about the current state of my love life. With a sigh I walked
up the four flights of dimly lit stairs to my apartment. Surprisingly
enough, when I entered, no one and nothing out of the ordinary greeted
me. No dead intern. No fairies with demands.

And most surprising of all, no one intent on a Blue barbecue.

"Huh," I said, wiping my loafers on the electrostatic mat on the
floor just inside the door. Sparks crackled from my body to the mat.
When the buzzing stopped, I headed forward, not too surprised to
find Right and Left conducting a military-style search of my apartment for intruders. I decided to let them have their winged way. For
the moment.

With great interest I headed to the kitchen and my refrigerator. I
pictured the bounty of goodies inside, all bought and paid for with
my own money. Money I'd made through a semi-honest living. It
wasn't bad to be Blue.

Until I opened the fridge door and remembered two things—first,
my maid had done all the grocery shopping, and second, she'd quit
more than two weeks ago, which explained the day-old coffee and
moldy bread from this morning. I slammed the refrigerator's door,
nearly toppling it in the process. "Damn it," I yelled as a bolt of low-
blood-sugar-induced electricity shot from my fingers, burning a hole
in the cheap kitchen countertop. I smacked out the burning embers
and then blew on my now aching hand.

So it wasn't good to be Blue either.

Tossing open the cabinet under the sink, I yanked out a bottle of
relatively expensive whiskey and poured a healthy dose in an eight-
ounce glass. I downed the first glass and poured a second. I vowed to
savor this one, mostly because the first nip had gone straight from my
very empty belly to my now even emptier head. I sat down on a chair,
waiting for the effects to pass. When they did I pulled out my cell
phone and dialed a number I found myself calling much too often in
times like this.

"Fairy of India, how can I help you?" a guy answered in a distinc-
tively nonaccented voice.

I sighed. "I'd like three orders of beef *saag* and a steak. Rare."

"You got it, pal," he said, adding to my already growing suspicion that Fairy of India wasn't as authentic as one might suspect. After giving him my credit card number I hung up and started sorting through a week's worth of mail. The Internet made two things more easily ignored—snail mail and normal pornography. Neither of which appealed to me much. I liked shock value.

And I got it as I read the envelope addressed only to "Reynolds." Not uncommon, but something about the fancy scrawled handwriting bothered me. The return address was the clincher, though—101 Police Plaza, New Never City Jail.

The implanted tooth that replaced the one viciously torn from my mouth last year by a violent psychopath started to ache. I tossed the envelope and whatever evil it contained into the trash. Then, merely as a safety precaution, I staggered to my feet and to the kitchen sink to wash my hands again and again until my doorbell rang thirty minutes later. I quickly dried my chapped palms with the nearest dish towel, which turned out to be an undershirt I'd worn two weeks ago, and went to answer the door, my stomach now much less excited by the heavenly scent rising from the hallway.

I opened the door to pay the delivery guy, who wore a red bindi in the center of his forehead and a shapely pair of wings on his back. Considering the red dot was traditionally worn only by women and symbolized love and honor, neither of which were my strong points, I decided to keep our interaction as short as possible. I just wanted my steak and spicy creamed spinach.

Once our transaction was complete and my hands were full of take-out containers, I kicked the door closed and dropped the food on the coffee table in front of my couch. I sat down, kicked off my loafers, and flipped on the TV with a slightly melted remote. Picking up the closest lukewarm box, I inhaled the scent of curry and spice, sighing happily before stabbing it with my index finger. Thirty seconds later the *saag* was piping hot. Who needed a microwave when one could conduct electricity? I grinned, and for the first time in two days, I started to relax.

CHAPTER 11

The next morning I shot awake with a silent scream. Acid rolled in my gut thanks to vivid images of James's charred corpse and the three-fourths of a fifth of whiskey I had consumed before bed. I took a shallow breath, suppressing the urge to jump out of bed and run to the toilet to puke. My longing to toss my steak-laden cookies increased when I caught sight of the two winged dudes on either side of my bed, silently standing guard while I slept.

The very thought creeped me out to no end.

"What the fuck?" I said, throwing my pillow at Right, who stood on the left of my bed, next to my nightstand. "Don't you guys sleep?"

Left, apparently the spokesman for the two, answered in a surprisingly deep voice for a guy barely thirty-six inches tall. "Not while we're on the job."

"Easy enough to remedy," I said. "You're fired. Now, get the hell out of my apartment."

He shook his chubby head. "You cannot fire us. Only the Tooth Fairy holds that power." His eyes narrowed on my face as his lip lifted into a smirk. "And *she* wants you alive; therefore, we will keep you that way, by whatever means necessary."

I laughed and then instantly regretted it. My head, already pounding to a different beat, now felt like a marching band tapping double time to an eighties heavy-metal song. "Is that a threat?" I asked, once the hammering inside my skull subsided a bit. Before he could respond, the full weight of his words slammed into me and anger rocketed through me. "Izzy is *not* the Tooth Fairy. Those days are over. The sooner you guys get that through your heads, the better." To them, once a Tooth Fairy, always a Tooth Fairy.

Until death did her wings part.

And I wasn't about to let that happen.

Left smiled at me like I was a clueless child asking how babies were made. "If you say so."

A flash of electrical anger zapped through my body, exiting my left foot. It shot into the ceiling, leaving a small scorch mark in its wake. I took a calming breath. It was too early and I was much too hungover for this shit.

Besides, I had work to do.

Foremost on my mind was finding out what my former Tooth Fairy of a partner had been looking for in my office the other night. Asking her would have to wait, though.

I would have to bide my time, waiting for the perfect moment to confront Izzy.

Clayton's fund-raiser tonight seemed just right.

Since I had ten or so hours until the gala, I decided to scrounge up some possible leads on James's murder. The best place to start was James himself. According to our employment records, he had resided on the edge of Fairyland with a gaggle of college-aged roommates, so as much as it pained me, and it truly did hurt, I got dressed, stopped off for an extra-large coffee and a bottle of aspirin from the local bodega, and flagged down a taxi to take me into the pit of hell also known as Fairyland.

Right and Left stayed glued to me, and yet, instead of being annoyed by their now somewhat ripe presence, I figured having the two winged guys by my side might actually work in my favor. For once. Under normal circumstances I was Blue non grata to the fairies. Since I'd nearly destroyed their entire population.

Bunch of winged, tiny, grudge-holding babies.

To top it off they believed I had somehow brainwashed their Tooth Fairy, forcing her from her rightful toothy obligation and into my world of deadbeats and lawyers. Like anyone could force Izzy into doing anything. I'd seen her with a gun to her head and she hadn't batted an eyelash. My partner was no pushover.

Until it came to those she loved.

Then she would die to protect each and every winged one of them.

I hoped like hell it never came to that.

For both our sakes.

CHAPTER 12

The cab pulled to the curb in front of a small row house on the outskirts of Fairyland known as Fraternity Row, Row, Row. The frat house was surprisingly easy to find. You just had to follow the yellow brick road and the stench of rotten cabbage. Luckily no one dropped a house on us, but we did run into a prince wearing skinny jeans, which was much worse.

James's former home looked unloved, with the shutters loosely hanging on rusted hinges, slamming against the house in the breeze. Peeling, weather-worn paint graced the structure, as did beer cans. They lay everywhere, as if a part of a science experiment that had gone wrong. A lounge chair sat on the rickety porch, along with an old-fashioned claw-foot bathtub. Of course both were full of empty beer cans. Above the door was a small engraved sign with the Greek lettering of some fraternity name.

"Something tells me we're not in Kansas anymore," I said with a halfhearted smile to the two winged dwarfs flanking my sides. While they didn't outright laugh at my joke, Right's eye did give a tiny twitch, a sure sign he was laughing on the inside.

I knocked on the wooden doorframe, fearing what would happen if I touched the rotted door. When only the faint sound of coughing reached my ears, I knocked again. Harder this time. Still no one answered. For a brief moment I wondered if James's death wasn't an attempt on my life as I first suspected. What if, as I stood on the porch, the killer was inside destroying the evidence of his crimes and/or murdering James's roommates?

Hell with that, I thought as I slammed the heel of my boot into the rotted wood of the door. It splintered inward, and a smell so foul I backed up a step oozed from the opening. My eyes began to water as

I waved a hand in front of my face to dispel the putrid air. At least James's roommates weren't dead as I'd first thought. Even decaying flesh didn't stink that bad.

Aw, the joys of college life.

"Dude," a drunken guy with a Fairyland U T-shirt on said as he stumbled toward me. "The door was unlocked."

Oops. "My bad," I said with a wince. Blue's PI rule number one—always check to make sure a door is locked first. Rule two had something to do with getting payment up front from any client with wings.

Drunk guy didn't seem to notice my heartfelt apology. Or he just didn't care. Either way, he took an unsteady swing at me, missing by a good six inches. The momentum of the punch carried him by me, and he ended up facefirst in the beer-can-filled bathtub. I might've felt sorry for the guy had his punch been aimed at someone else. But it wasn't, so I did what any PI would do. I offered him a hand up.

As soon as his skin made contact with mine, he froze in electrified shock. Fifty thousand volts rushed through my body and into his. He jerked back, muscles constricting. I let go of his hand and he dropped back into the bathtub. Seeing as he wouldn't be of much help for at least the next ten minutes, I took matters into my own hands. Slowly I stepped through the broken doorway and into the hallway of the house. The smell inside was even worse than outside. Urine, beer, unwashed bodies, with a hint of rotten food and fairy dust, filled the air, making talking nearly impossible, let alone breathing.

Right seemed to share my opinion, for his face turned green two feet through the door. Left didn't last much longer. "Go," I said to both fairyguards. "Wait for me outside."

For once neither argued, nearly trampling each other in a race for the door. I watched them leave, a small rush of macho victory as well as bile rising in me. I wanted to throw up but decided it would only prolong my stay inside. "Hello," I called into the dimly lit interior.

A hacking wet cough answered.

I winced, swallowing hard as I stepped in something that squished much like decaying cat. I glanced down. Nope, not a cat. A rat. One the size of a small dog. I vowed to burn my boots as soon as I left this place, as well as the rest of my clothes, and possibly shave my head. I scraped the bits of dead rat from the bottom of my boot on the steps leading to the second floor.

The smoker's cough sounded again.

With a deep breath I charged forward through piles of debris, beer cans, and discarded undergarments. I reminded myself of why I was there in the first place. I owed James. If wading through garbage was penance for his death, then I would damn well do it with a smile on my face. Okay, not a smile, but I would do it nonetheless.

"Hello," I called again when I reached the top floor. "Is anyone here?"

The blessed scent of burning tobacco tickled my nostrils, lessening the other terrible aromas. I pushed open the door closest to me, not too surprised to see a bunch of young guys in various stages of undress and levels of drunken comas. All but one of the men were asleep. The only one awake waved a hand in front of his face to dispel the smoke between us. "Who are you?" he asked with yet another hacking cough.

"Blue Reynolds," I offered. "I'm here to ask you some questions about one of your roommates."

He scratched the side of his face, seemingly unconcerned that a blue-haired guy had busted into his house and wanted information about his roommates. "Which one?"

"James."

His forehead wrinkled. "What about him? He owe you money? You won't be getting it. Not from him."

I shook my head. "No, nothing like that. James interned for me. I came by to offer my condolences, and maybe check out his room?" And then get a tetanus shot, I added silently. A big one. The kind they used on the dragons they kept at the New Never City Zoo.

He eyed me up and down. "First and last months' rent."

"What?"

"You heard me," he said. "You want inside James's room, it's gonna cost you."

Having a guy, a kid really, shake me down wasn't on my list of favorite things. But I did want a peek into James's life. I wanted to know more about the kid who'd died in my place. I wanted to know if he had family, if they loved him, or if he, like me, had been alone in the world. Not that it mattered. Nothing I learned or did would bring the poor kid back. "Fine," I said, pulling out my wallet. "How much?"

He glanced at me, then at my wallet, and finally at my boots. Most likely assessing how much he could get me to pay. My thuggish good looks paid off for once as he said, "Two hundred."

"Deal." I passed over a one-hundred-dollar bill along with five twenties. Some days it was nice to have an expense account to afford such luxuries as bribes to stoned college kids. "Which room was his?"

"Third door on your left."

I nodded, closing the door behind me after I left. I vowed right there and then that if I ever had kids, they sure as hell wouldn't go to college. The thought of bringing a child into the world scared me nearly as much as the image of the baby that flashed through my mind.

A blue-haired baby.

With pink wings.

CHAPTER 13

My luck had changed, I thought as I pushed open the door to James's room—a clean and tidy albeit small room with a thin layer of dust on the dresser and bookcase. No beer cans here. Or if there had been, they weren't here anymore. In fact the room seemed a little too clean. A little too sparse. It felt unlived-in, as if James had never existed at all. My eyes narrowed. Had someone cleaned up after learning of James's murder?

Maybe James was just a tidy housekeeper? Not that I'd ever seen any signs of latent cleanliness. Hell, the kid's desk was littered with files, paperwork, and discarded fast-food bags. I shook my head to dispel the hint of paranoia.

Taking a deep, clean-smelling breath, I began my search. For what, I didn't know, but everyone, even a college student, had secrets. A black-and-white photograph of a young woman with light-colored hair, her face obscured slightly by the glare of afternoon sun, sat on the nightstand by the bed. I picked it up, examining it closely. Was this James's first love? Had they planned a future together? A future he would now never have? Guilt filled me once again, reminding me just how responsible I was for his death.

It should've been me.

James should be in my room staring at a picture of my sweetheart.

Except I was still very much alive, and I never had nor would have a future with any woman. Not until I found a way to cure my electrical curse. After all, what woman in her right mind would marry a lightning rod? For a brief second Izzy's face flashed through my mind. I set the picture down a little harder than necessary. The frame shattered under the pressure, sending shards of glass raining down. I winced as a fragment sliced into my palm.

Just desserts, I supposed.

Blood from the wound dripped onto the photograph. I pulled it free from the broken frame and stuffed it into my pocket for safekeeping. One day I would find this young woman, for James's sake. I would act as if I knew him, tell her what a good guy he'd been. Maybe even make up a story or two about how he'd solved an impossible case. And maybe he would've.

If some bastard hadn't staged an "accident" for me.

Pressing the sleeve of my shirt against the bleeding cut on my hand, I finished my search of the room. Nothing else caught my eye. James was a normal college kid with big dreams. He wore jeans and T-shirts. Spent his days working for college credit. And died doing the same. With a heavy sadness in my chest, I left the room, quietly closing the door behind me. Almost but not quite the closure I needed.

Closure I wouldn't have until justice was served.

An eye for an eye.

Or in this case, a fry for a fry.

Since I was already on the outskirts of Fairyland, I decided to do a quick search for the missing fairies. When in Rome, after all. Except Fairyland smelled much more like stale Chinese food and day-old fairy dust. Right and Left's attitude seemed to instantly change as soon as we hit the streets of Fairyland. They went from watchful and sullen to cracking the occasional smile. On top of that, they even pointed out a few historical landmarks, like oddly weaponized tour guides.

But the deeper we moved into Fairyland and the happier they became, the unhappier I was. I stood out like a blue-haired thumb. Not only was I about three feet taller than everyone on the street, but every fairy in the district knew of my role in Izzy's leaving her toothier duties. And blamed me for the same.

I tensed when a group of heavily tattooed fairies stepped from a fairy bar on the corner. They were loud, and quite drunk, even at eleven in the morning. Considering my sober state, I felt compelled to judge them for their debauchery. I damn well wanted to be half in the bag, but no, I was stuck in Fairyland searching for missing fairies, who'd probably bite my kneecaps if I ever found them. Some days it paid to stay in bed.

"It's him." Two of the bigger, drunker fairies pointed at me, their wings in full flutter. Dust flew in all directions. A bad sign. I wasn't looking for a fight. Hell, the last thing I needed right now was to electrocute a bunch of winged devils.

But I would if it came down to it.

I smiled at the thought as electrical current arced through me.

Right must've noticed my sudden glee, for he grabbed my arm, shocking us both, him literally as well as in a more figurative sense. "Ow," he complained, releasing my arm.

I winced. "Sorry about that."

"You'll be sorrier if we don't leave right now," he said, motioning to a growing and equally angry mob of fairies. There must've been fifty of them, wings aflutter. A toxic cloud of fairy dust rose from the group, indicating my peril. As much as I wanted to stay and electrocute the boisterous lot of them, Right was right. I hadn't come to Fairyland to cause a riot. I was here to actually help the winged degenerates now throwing rocks my way.

When a rock nicked the side of my face, I allowed Right and Left to hustle me away from danger. Which was easier said than done, as the crowd now reached into the hundreds. Didn't fairies work? Then it hit me. Today was Fairy Independence Day, the same day, more than a hundred years ago, that the first Isabella Davis, Izzy's great-grandmother, had freed the fairies from their Shadows.

I shook my head. No wonder these guys were so fired up, not to mention three wings to the wind. I should've guessed. Clayton was one smart fairy. He couldn't have picked a better day to hold his fund-raiser; add in Izzy, the great-granddaughter of Isabella the first, and the former Tooth Fairy to boot, and he'd rake in the campaign contributions tonight.

No way in hell would I let him use Izzy again.

Not while there was electricity still left in my body.

Not too surprisingly, the rest of my day in Fairyland didn't go much better than the first part. Every nondrunken fairy I approached claimed no knowledge of anything amiss in Fairyland, let alone a rash of missing compatriots. And every drunken fairy tried to knock my teeth in, and usually wound up rocked by fifty thousand volts for their trouble.

Right and Left proved useless to boot.

They didn't even try to protect me from those drunken attacks.

When I said as much, holding a hand to the bite wound on my thigh, Right just looked at me and smiled. "Isabella asked us to protect you from death."

I frowned. "So why aren't you helping me?"

"She didn't say anything about stopping you from getting a well-deserved ass kicking."

"Fair enough," I said, shocking a fairy with orange wings and equally bright carrot-colored eyebrows who was leaping up and down, trying to punch me in the teeth. His small body went rigid, and then he dropped to the concrete. I stepped over him, continuing on my quest to find any fairy willing to talk to me.

CHAPTER 14

Three hours later, after a few attempts to learn anything from the fairies, I blew out a sigh along with a stream of cigarette smoke. I'd approached at least fifty fairies, but not one would talk to me, let alone discuss what they considered fairy business. I was an outsider. I always had been, and I always would be. Most of the time this fact didn't bother me. I liked being a lone wolf. But I needed help to find the missing fairies before someone dusted them to death. Since the fairies weren't talking, I had to think outside the fairy box.

That left me with one alternative. And not a good one at that. There was only one person in all of New Never City with her sheep in every dirty deal—Little Bo Peep. Considering our history, calling her for information wasn't the brightest move.

But Bo was a businesswoman at heart. She would sell her entire flock to a slaughterhouse for the right price. While her greedy nature made for a less-than-pleasant friendship, it worked in my favor when it came to buying intel.

With one small exception.

Bo Peep refused to answer any questions about my past. About who I was or where my electrical curse had come from. That, in itself, pissed me off; then add in her selling me out to the leader of the Shadows and his minions last year, which very nearly resulted in my death, and we weren't on the best of terms. But I had a pocket full of cash and a desire for what only Bo could provide—as long as I didn't turn my back, for I was fairly sure she'd plunge the closest sharpened object between my shoulder blades without a second thought.

Crushing my cigarette under the heel of my boot, I pulled out my cell phone, preparing to call Bo Peep. Before I could start to dial, my phone gave a shrill ring. I jerked up, nearly dropping the phone before I checked the caller ID.

Bo Peep's name and number flashed across the screen.

"What the hell?" I said to myself, and then answered the call. "Bo?" I asked in lieu of greeting, my voice only slightly unsteady. Was Peep some kind of mind reader? I shuddered at the thought.

"Well, well, Blue Reynolds, it's been a while," her voice slithered through the line.

Ignoring her comment, I said, "What do you want?"

She laughed. "What? No, 'Hi, Bo, how are you? How's the flock?' I thought we were friends."

It was my turn to laugh. "How about, what the hell do you want?"

"I'm hurt," she said sounding anything but. "Remember the fun we used to have together?" I remembered some electrically charged encounters, two of which left me with rug burns in various places and no ready explanation for how they'd gotten there. But that was a long time ago. I was no longer the same guy. I'd matured. "I remember a lot of things . . ."

"Do I have to apologize?" she purred. "You know how much I hate to say I'm sorry."

I laughed. "Not nearly as much as I hate getting the shit beat out of me because you sold me down the Hansel River."

"Aww, did Blue get a boo-boo?"

"Cut the shit, Bo. What do you want?"

"It's not what I want . . ." She gave a small, husky laugh. "Come to my place and I'll give you just what you need," she said in a silken whisper, and my blood detoured south to my nether, blue-haired regions. It was the last place I wanted to be warmed by Bo Peep.

I cleared my throat. "I don't think that's a good idea."

"Probably not," she said. "But it is the only way I'll tell you what happened to your little friend. You know . . . the extra-crispy one."

Even as I boarded the elevator that would whisk me to Bo Peep's penthouse apartment in the sky, I shook my head, knowing full well whatever was about to happen wouldn't bode well for my physical and likely mental health. Thankfully I'd managed to ditch Right and Left in Fairyland an hour earlier, so there would be no witnesses to my downward spiral. For fairyguards, the two were pretty damn easy to ditch. I simply pointed up the street, said, "Is that a molar?" and took off in the opposite direction.

The elevator dinged, and I straightened to my full height. I rubbed my fingers together, generating enough of a spark to fry whatever Peep had lying in wait. With a whoosh the doors opened in a luxurious and expensively decorated penthouse apartment. Floor-to-ceiling windows reflected the orange glow of the sunset over the city below, showering the room in streaks of gold. The intense beauty had nothing on the woman standing in front of me. Little Bo Peep was everything a man could want in a woman—platinum blond straight from the bottle, stacked, and with questionable morals. She wore her hair long, curling around her shoulders. Bare shoulders.

To go along with the bare rest of her.

I blew out a shallow breath, trying my damnedest to tear my gaze from the lush swells of her tanned body.

"What took you so long? I was beginning to worry," she said, motioning me past her nakedness and into the penthouse. I stepped out of the elevator, careful to avoid brushing any part of my body against hers. My bluish arm hair rose with electricity and more than a little lust. Thankfully, for the moment, the hairs were the only things to rise to attention. Giving in to lust wasn't a great idea, not with Bo. I needed to keep my head if I wanted to get out of here alive. "Can I get you a drink?" she asked, motioning to an array of dark-colored liquor bottles. "A forty-year-old scotch, perhaps?"

"I'm not here for a drink."

Her mouth lifted into a sultry smirk. "Just what are you here for, Blue?"

"Answers would be nice." I walked to the window, more to take my mind off what Bo was so kindly offering than because of a desire to study the cityscape below, even if both views were spectacular. I stared down at the people scurrying home after a long day a hundred stories below. In that moment I felt like a part of something rather than apart from it. I turned back to the very naked Bo Peep. "What do you know about James's death?"

She shook her finger at me. "Foreplay first, Blue. You know my rules."

I grinned, reaching into my pants to give her what she wanted.

Her eyes grew hot, and she wetted her lips, which glistened like rubies in the fading light.

"Two grand enough?" I pulled my wallet out, counting the bills I'd pulled out of the ATM under her watchful, greedy gaze. When I had the right amount I waved it toward her. She made no move to take it. My suspicion immediately mounted as my eyes narrowed. "What's your game, Bo?"

She sighed, long and loud, making sounds almost like a moans of pleasure. "We used to be friends. I miss that." Her eyes burned into mine as if her intensity would be enough to convince me that she was telling the truth. Hell, I had my doubts that Bo knew what honesty was, let alone how to wield it. "I miss you," she said with a pretty, single tear glimmering in her eye.

"And yet you betrayed me." I shrugged, ignoring her tears and the way her breasts rose and fell with her every breath. The latter was a little more difficult to dismiss, but I managed to do so before I lost my head and took her to bed. I cleared my throat. "Can't say I'm real interested in reliving our past."

A frown marred her otherwise perfect features, the first genuine emotion to cross her face since I walked into the room. "This is about her, isn't it?"

"Her?"

She laughed with a surprising amount of bitterness. "You damn well know I'm talking about Isabella, your little fairy girlfriend. She's ruined you, Blue."

"Excuse me?"

She took two steps forward, her hips swaying in a hypnotic beat. "You used to be fun."

"Not that I don't trust your motives," I said sarcastically, "but your sudden concern for my merriment makes me wonder."

Her eyelashes fluttered prettily. "About?"

"Why am I here?"

"Fine," she said, grabbing a crimson silk robe from the back of a shiny leather sofa. She wrapped it around her, tying the sash tightly before answering. "I wanted to apologize for that thing that happened . . . you know . . . with the Shadows . . ."

"You mean the trying-to-murder-me thing?" For a very brief second I wondered if Bo was the blond woman the Ferns claimed to have seen discussing my murder. As quickly as the thought crossed my mind, I dismissed it. Bo wasn't the type to be seen in a dive fairy bar.

She was much more likely to hire a killer out of the back of a fashion magazine.

She gave an exaggerated eye roll, one that did nothing to diminish her looks. "Don't be a drama queen. You're still alive . . ."

". . . and you got paid," I finished for her. "If you really want to make things right, you'll have to answer a question for me. With complete honesty." I paused, enjoying her game for the first time since I'd arrived. "And for free."

"Blue," she said. Her tongue darted out, licking her lips. "Some things you are better off never knowing. It's for your own good. Trust me."

Trust her? Yeah, right. I held up my hand. "I was talking about James's murder, Bo. Not my past." As moments ticked by in silence, I had a sneaking suspicion I wasn't here by accident. Bo Peep wanted something from me, something other than the cash in my pocket.

What exactly, I wasn't sure.

I gazed deeply into her lying eyes. "You have no idea who killed James, do you?"

She shrugged. "I know more than you think. Don't make the mistake of assuming otherwise."

The mistake I'd made had nothing to do with thinking, but rather the woman standing so close to me, which was easy enough to fix. "You're setting me up. Again." I reached for her arm, my fingers digging into the muscle of her upper arm. "Why?"

She shrieked as electricity shot through her. Not enough to do actual harm; just enough to warn her that I wasn't messing around. Whatever she was cooking up wasn't going to work. Instead of pushing me away, she stepped into my arms, her breasts pressing against my chest. The thin fabric of her silk robe was little protection for either of us. Sparks shot between us, heating the air and my body parts.

She wrapped her arms around my neck, dragging my mouth to hers. I tried to resist, to pull back—at least that's what I later told myself—but I was unable to stop the flare of heat crackling through me. It had been much too long. And she felt so wrong in my arms. The kind of wrong a man was unable to escape without serious damage.

Our lips melded into a power-hungry kiss. Her tongue brushed mine as her hand slid down my backside. I reacted as expected, deepening what already felt like a consuming kiss. She tasted like sin with a hint of sheep. An oddly tempting sensation. I pressed my knee between her bare legs, feeling the heat of her through the fabric of my pants. She moaned low and deep in her throat, urging me on.

Behind us the elevator dinged.

The doors opened as I tore my mouth from hers.

My gaze flew to the three shadowy figures across the room.

Bo let out a calculated laugh. "I believe you know our guests."

I closed my eyes and swore. Would I ever fucking learn?

CHAPTER 15

"Izzy, wait," I yelled as my partner and her two fairy minions, Right and Left, disappeared behind the closing elevator doors. The look on her face when she saw Bo in my arms would be one I would remember for a lifetime.

Izzy had looked completely . . . unaffected. Not that I expected anything more. We were just partners, after all.

She'd simply raised a flame-colored eyebrow, stepped back into the elevator, and vanished to the floors below. There was no surprise or shock on her face. Nothing but acceptance, as if she'd expected no more from the likes of Blue Reynolds.

But I wasn't *that* Blue Reynolds anymore.

Or was I? I glanced down at Bo's rounded breasts, barely covered by her robe. I'd known what would very likely happen if I came here. Well, I'd expected a little bloodshed too, but maybe she was saving it for later. I dropped my arms, stepping away from Bo as if she was diseased; given her obsession with her sheep, I suspected a case of fleas at the very least.

"What's the matter?" she asked, her eyes alight with mischief and more than a hint of malice. The same look I'd long associated with Bo. I should've known better. I cursed myself for a fool. "Tooth Fairy got your tongue along with your balls?" She held out her manicured nails, examining each bloodred tip. "I hear she keeps them in her purse."

I wasn't about to fall for Bo's baiting, not again. "Did you get what you wanted?" I asked, my voice filled with barely controlled rage. Flecks of static electricity crackled in the air. But I wouldn't lose control. "What was the plan? Izzy walks in on you and me, and what? She ends our partnership? She stabs me with a toothbrush? What?"

Bo licked her lips. "You don't need her. Without her interference you can be the man you are meant to be." She reached for my arm, but I pulled back before I caused real harm. I'd done enough as it was. "Give us a chance," she said. "With your insider knowledge of your clients and my savvy, we can make a pile of money, and in the end, we will rule this city. You and I. Together."

"You and I, huh?"

Her lips lifted into a stunning and sexy smile. She ran her finger down her robe, dipping into her nakedness with the promise of a million earthly delights. "Yes. Us."

I laughed but without humor. "I'd rather screw a light socket."

With that parting shot, I walked across the room and pressed the elevator call button. Not the smoothest of exits, but I was merely a man, a man who sure as hell didn't want to walk down a hundred flights of stairs. The elevator finally arrived, and I stepped in, not once looking at Bo.

As the elevator doors slipped shut, the faint scent of fairy dust and what smelled like the sea brushed over my senses. I pictured Izzy and her utter lack of emotion. My chest gave a small squeeze in response. Great. On top of a dead intern, I now had heart disease.

Sometimes life just wasn't fair.

The unfairness of it all faded as I headed back to my apartment. I'd known better. Bo wasn't hard to read. She did whatever it took to get what she wanted in the end. Nothing was ever what it seemed when she was around. I vowed to avoid playing her hide-and-sheep games from then on.

After a thirty-minute hike to my apartment, my anger had receded along with the pull of lust in my loins. I'd just have to tell Izzy the truth, that nothing had happened between Bo and me, that I'd gone to pump her for information, and not for anything else. Not that Izzy would believe me. After all, she had little reason to believe that I'd changed. That I'd matured. But I had, damn it! The last hour aside.

Tossing the half-smoked cigarette into the street, I entered my apartment building and climbed the four flights of stairs to my apartment. The faint twitter of bells and music reached my ears as I pressed my key into the lock on my door.

Before I could open the lock, the door flew inward, as did my entire body. I tried to catch myself but ended up tripping over the electrostatic mat on the floor and landing facefirst on the hardwood. The sticky residue of melted rock salt scraped against my cheek as the faint aroma of charred intern burned into the floorboards assaulted my nostrils.

I quickly leapt to my feet, expecting a jolt of electricity beyond any I'd known to rocket through my body. When nothing happened, I let out a shallow breath and looked around the apartment for whoever had opened the door. I was surprised and pleased to see a set of pink wings.

"Izzy," I began. "I'm so glad—"

She cut me off. "We have to leave in an hour for Clayton's fundraiser. I brought you something to wear . . ." She held out a black tuxedo, the same style worn by dapper spies who liked shaken martinis.

"You didn't have to—"

She snorted. "Oh, but I did. We all know how busy you are . . ."

"I can explain. Bo said she—"

"If you want to make a fool of yourself again, I couldn't care less. What and who you do are your business." She threw the tuxedo on the couch, her actions at odds with her words. "I'm going home to get ready for the gala." She paused, looking me up and down. "Unless you asked Bo Peep to be your date."

"Damn it, Izzy. It wasn't like I planned—"

She held up her hand to cut me off. "I'll expect you in one hour, unless, of course, you accidently fall on top of another naked woman."

I raised an eyebrow at her snarky statement.

She smiled, showing off sharp white teeth. "But what are the odds of that happening twice in a five-hour span?"

Sixty-forty at best.

Unless there was a storm brewing.

In that case my odds went up considerably.

I decided not to share the over/under with Izzy yet.

It was best to sometimes just let it ride.

CHAPTER 16

Exactly one hour later, a bright yellow taxi pulled up to the curb in front of Izzy's brownstone uptown, and I leapt out, waving to Right and Left, who had followed in another taxi. Both fairyguards held up a hand, raising their stubby middle fingers. Guess the little guys held a grudge for my ditching them earlier. Not like I cared one way or another. I would do what I pleased, when I pleased. If they couldn't keep up, that was their problem.

I rapped on the front door, surprised when Izzy opened it immediately. I took a step back, both for balance and to take in the full effect of the stunning vision of half-fairy in front of me. Izzy wore a strapless black dress that fell to her trim ankles, flaring in all the right places. Her hair hung loosely around her shoulders in waves of auburn fire. But it was her full, plump, ruby-colored lips that drew my gaze again and again.

And her wings, of course.

They fluttered lightly in the breeze, sparkling like beacons of light in the night.

Heat filled my lower body, tensing every muscle with electricity and lust. Breathe through it, I ordered my treacherous libido. No matter how delicious Izzy looked, she was off-limits. My partner, I reminded myself. Even if she wasn't, we could never be together. My curse all but guaranteed it. For the slightest of my touches would cause her pain. And I would never be able to resist touching Izzy if allowed the chance.

"Is it that bad?" she asked, running a nervous hand down her dress. "I should change." She spun on her ruby-slippered heel and headed back inside. I tried to stop her, but the flash of the pale white skin down her back claimed my ability to speak. I could only stand there waiting for my blood to return to my head. When I was able to form words again, very basic ones at that, I followed her into her brownstone. "Izzy," I called. "You look amazing. Please don't change."

She stepped from her bedroom, her lips puckered as if she didn't believe me, let alone a word I ever said. "Are you sure? It isn't too . . ." Too perfect? Too breathtaking? Too bad she was my partner? I shook my head, afraid I just might drop to my knees and start to beg for a crumb of affection.

She pulled at the fabric above her barely contained breasts. "This dress was not made for wings." I disagreed but thought it best not to voice my opinion.

For a moment she looked vulnerable and much younger than her twenty-seven years. The need to protect her took me by surprise. Izzy didn't need protection. She could and would take care of any danger that came her way. I stifled the outrageous desire and held out my gloved hand. "Let's get this shit over with," I said with a grin. Hesitating for only a second, she took my hand in hers, and together we headed off to the ball. Thankfully not one godmother—fairy or otherwise—screamed out a ridiculous curfew as the taxi shot down the street.

A few minutes into the taxi ride Izzy's cell phone buzzed. She glanced down at the caller ID, her mouth curving into a frown. "It's Jonas," she said to me. "I wonder what he wants." Instead of waiting for whatever witty commentary I came up with, she answered the call. "Is something wrong?" Silence filled the cab as she listened intently, the fingers of her free hand curling into a fist as her eyes grew violet with rage.

Whatever Jonas was telling her wasn't good. My heart rate increased as the silence grew.

"How bad is it?' she asked a few seconds before she hung up. She turned to me, her lips a thin, flat line.

I swallowed. "What happened?"

"A fire." She paused as if weighing her words. "At the office. Two and a half hours ago."

The hairs on the back of my neck danced with electrical current. "Was anyone hurt?"

She shook her head. "Thankfully, no. No one was inside. I was the last person to leave after Right and Left came to tell me you'd gone missing."

"How bad is the damage?"

She frowned, her eyes steady on the traffic outside the window of the cab. "Jonas says it was contained to only one office."

"That's gre—"

"Not really. It was your office, Blue." She turned back to face me, wincing slightly. "Someone set fire to your office."

CHAPTER 17

The fire put a damper on the evening, but there was nothing either of us could do about it tonight. Tomorrow we'd contact the insurance company and deal with the rest of the fire-related mess. Besides, we had a more pressing problem tonight. Even though most of the fairies adored Izzy, a small faction loyal to the Fairy Council had slightly less admiration. So much so, they'd vowed to destroy her. I wasn't too worried, but I wasn't a fool either. Every moment Izzy spent at Clayton's fund-raiser was a chance for those winged and nonwinged assholes to make good on their threat. I wouldn't let that happen. Not as long as my heart beat with electrical current. Nobody would hurt a feather on her wings.

Even me.

"Behave tonight. This is a big night and Clayton needs our support," Izzy said as the cab pulled in front of the hotel. I nodded once, not bothering to voice my concerns again. Izzy had made up her mind to come to the fund-raiser tonight, and nothing I said would make a difference. And I'd said quite a bit when she'd first brought the subject up. Most of what was said was said with words foul enough to make three men in a tub blush. Yet, in the end, I'd reluctantly agreed to attend the fund-raiser, even offering to donate in the form of not frying Clayton on his big night.

The cab stopped outside the infamous Fairyland Hotel, the same place where the Fairy Pack used to do all their hard drinking and even harder hookering. A valet in a tiny tuxedo opened Izzy's door, helping her from the taxi while doing his best not to drool on the bottom of her gown. I couldn't fault the little winged devil. Izzy looked that good.

"Madam Tooth Fairy," the valet gushed, his chubby cheeks growing red as he stammered, "it is an honor. If you need anything—"

"She doesn't," I said, hoping to ward off the inevitable awkward fairy-removal process, which included a crowbar and enough electrical current to light half the city. "But if she did"—I paused, waiting for the little guy to tear his gaze off Izzy's loveliness and redirect it into my warning glare—"I'm the one who will get it. Got it?"

The little guy released Izzy's kneecap as he snapped to attention. "Yes, sir."

Izzy raised a flame-colored eyebrow but spoke softly enough that only I could hear her. "*She* doesn't need anyone, especially *you*, to play bodyguard. Do *I* make myself clear?"

Izzy was kidding herself if, even for a second, she thought I was there for any other reason than to watch her back. I'd rather have my teeth ripped out with a pair of golden pliers than spend two minutes at this fairy circus, let alone with the twins and their cronies. But she needed my protection, whether she knew it or not, if not from the throng of winged dwarfs decked out in their finest duds, at least from her own uncanny ability to land straight into whatever fairy-related craziness was currently plaguing Fairyland. You could take the fairy out of Fairyland . . .

"I mean it, Blue," she hissed when I didn't respond. "Don't push me. Not tonight."

I winked at her as I reached into my pocket for a few bills. I pressed them into the valet's tiny palm, hoping it would encourage him to release his death grip on the folds of Izzy's gown before I had to fry him away. "Thanks."

The winged valet looked at the money and then at Izzy, as if, to top off all her whispered achievements, including walking on water, she'd single-handedly fed his tiny family for a month. Forget the guy who actually handed over his own hard-earned cash.

Fucking fairies.

"Have a nice evening," he said, finally letting go of Izzy, though with reluctance. I took the opportunity to sweep her through the hotel doors and into the chaos inside the hotel. The crowd inside the lobby parted like the legs of a princess on prom night, all eyes locked on the beauty on my arm.

Even though I was there only to keep Izzy safe, warmth rushed up my spine, and not the electrical kind. I felt pride, in myself, and in what Izzy and I had accomplished over the last year. We'd worked hard to make the company a go, learning to work with each other. But also, deep within my primitive and not-so-primitive brain, I felt unfettered possession.

But Izzy wasn't mine.

Not in that way.

And she never would be.

CHAPTER 18

"Isabella," Clayton called, holding his fleshy arms wide. "You look absolutely amazing."

Izzy smiled at the much shorter man, leaning down so he could kiss her cheeks. His lips made smacking noises when he touched her skin. "You look quite handsome too." She ran a hand down his tiny bright-lime-colored tuxedo, which I had to admit didn't look nearly as dumb as it should have on a two-foot-tall guy. That probably had something to do with the vibrant color of his wings. I tilted my head, studying the vivid hue.

Clayton had dyed his wings.

I shook my head, embarrassed for him as well as all of fairykind. Fucking fairy politics at work. To become the next Tooth Fairy, Clayton had made many sacrifices, from dying his wings to kissing up to Big Mouthwash. The whole process was out of hand. But Izzy insisted when she'd first stepped down as the Tooth Fairy that the fairies embrace a completely democratic election. No more would the toothy torch/curse be appointed by the council. And then thanks to the ruling on Fairies United, money and big business now ruled all aspects of the Tooth Fairy game.

"Emerson is here. He's offered a significant contribution." Clayton's greedy gaze grew even greedier as his wings flapped with excitement. "I told Richard that you'd stop by his table. He has a check, but he will only give it to you. Then you must meet—"

I grabbed Clayton by the throat, cutting him off with a small squeak. "Izzy is here as a guest. Not for show-and-tell. She's done enough for you already."

"Blue," she said, slapping at my hand on the now chartreuse-colored candidate. "Stop it." I released him but didn't like it one bit. Yet Izzy was far from finished berating me. "I offered to fund-raise for the campaign. You know that. Clayton will make a fine Tooth Fairy."

The winged imp straightened to his full height, which wasn't that impressive, as Izzy spoke. "Thank you, Isabella. I will make you proud." He then turned to me, wagging his finger in my face. "And you—the day I'm elected Tooth Fairy, you better watch your bicuspids."

I grinned at his puny threat.

"Behave," Izzy said. "Both of you."

Clayton nodded, kissed her hand, and moved off to butter up another poor winged soul who'd wake up tomorrow regretting giving Clayton his hard-earned dough. Izzy turned to me, a smile hovering on her lips. "Try to be nice. Just for tonight."

I laughed loud enough to draw the attention of everyone within a ten-foot radius. "I was being nice. I let him go before he passed out."

She rolled her eyes, lowering her voice to a whisper. "There are a lot of important people here. People it would be good for us to get to know better."

"Is that so?"

"People with money."

Thanks to our partnership, we now had plenty of income. So what was Izzy's point? I waited for her to continue.

"And secrets," she whispered. "Ones they will pay to keep."

The corner of my lip lifted. "Are you thinking of a little blackmail?"

She laughed. "Of course not. I'm thinking about our company and its future." She paused, her eyes locked on mine. "Our future."

Before I could press her for more information, a crowd of eager groupies surrounded us. My hand hovered on Izzy's lower back, feeling the heat of her skin through the leather of my gloves, just in case her fan club turned ugly—or uglier than they already were. No matter what the fashion experts said, plunging necklines and cake-thick makeup were not a fairy's friends. The whole lot of them looked like rejects from a seventies movie.

While Izzy charmed the young and old fairies alike, I watched the crowd. Not hard to do when I towered over most of it by a good three feet. But I wasn't the only nonwinged species in attendance. The New Never City mayor stood with his entourage in the northwest corner, pressing the flesh like a good slimy politician. My skin crawled just looking at them. Representatives from all the unions were also present, including the newest boss of the Villainous Union. A guy I'd been hearing a lot about over the last month. A guy I vowed to stay far away from. A few celebrities with pinprick pupils and arm candy rounded out the group. Laughter filled the ballroom, mixed with pleas for campaign contributions and vile promises, like any good party.

Everyone seemed to be having a great time, their faces washed in the glow of expensive alcohol and finger foods. Everyone with the exception of the guy standing a few feet away, watching Izzy's every move, a murderous expression on his grumpy face.

CHAPTER 19

I glanced from Grumpy, the head of the Fairy Council, to Izzy and back again, weighing the anger burning in his eyes against the possibility that he would attack. The odds weren't in our favor. Even as I wanted nothing more than to snatch him up and toss his ass out of the gala, leaving Izzy alone for even a minute was against my better judgment. Grumpy wasn't her only enemy. In fact, he was one of six that I knew about, all members of the Fairy Council, who'd nearly lost everything when Izzy had insisted on a new democracy.

My eyes scanned the rest of the crowd for the other council members, not seeing any of them at the moment, but fairies and dwarfs, which were what the council was made up of, all looked alike to me.

Minus the wingspan.

I did, however, spot a familiar face in the crowd and let out a sigh. I supposed it could've been worse. I waved at Clark Boyer III, the newest member of team Reynolds, motioning him over. With a dip of his head he acknowledged my wild gesturing. Then he shook hands with each of the well-dressed politicians and celebrities surrounding him and headed our way. Every few feet someone would stop him. He would smile at them, showing off a full set of even, white, and expensive teeth as he listened intently to whatever crap they were saying, before he'd move on. Clark seemed to own the room, as if he'd been born into this world of power, wealth, and privilege. The Boyer name was synonymous with fancy parties and ass-kissing.

Much to my dismay it took Clark a full five minutes to make it to where Izzy and I stood. By that time Grumpy had disappeared.

"Reynolds, good to see—" he began.

"Watch her," I said, pushing Izzy his way. I didn't bother to glance back, my focus completely centered on finding and eliminating whatever malicious intent Grumpy and the other dwarfs might possess. I had a bad feeling about this—so bad, in fact, electrical current rose within me like a gathering storm.

I headed out of the ballroom, my gaze bouncing quickly back and forth. As I plunged through the thick crowd, not a single soul tried to stop me. I guess the winged set had learned a thing or two about getting in Blue Reynolds's way. Of course, I'd also learned a few things about large groups of fairies.

The little fiends liked to bite.

My knees still bore tooth marks from last year's mêlée.

After about twenty minutes of searching, I finally spotted the grumpy dwarf sitting in the hotel bar, away from the chaos of the crowds. A half-empty drink sat in front of him. My every instinct screamed trap, but I headed toward him without hesitation. These guys would not harm one red hair on Izzy's head, let alone ruin tonight for her. I would make sure of it.

"Have a seat, Blue Boy." Grumpy's stumpy leg kicked out the barstool next to him. I did as he asked, settling in and ordering a club soda with lime, a thirst-quenching but, more important, electrically conductive drink. If it came down to it, I would toss the drink on Grumpy and then apply a few thousand volts, ruining his day at the very least.

When the bartender set my drink down, Grumpy's lips lifted into a humorless smile. "We should've finished the job we started."

"And what job was that?" I asked, even though I knew he was referring to last year, when they'd tried desperately to have me killed. Good thing neither of us held a grudge.

He snorted. "That bitch ruined everything."

I pulled off one of my gloves in warning. "You were saying?"

His eyes shot from my bare fingers to my face and back again. "This democracy thing is a big mistake. Fairies aren't smart enough to elect the right Tooth Fairy. They will vote for whoever makes the most promises, and then what? We end up with a dirtbag like Clayton holding all the dentin. Fairyland can't survive with a fairy like him at the helm."

I shrugged. He did have a point. If I relied on a daily dose of dentin, Clayton's greed would give me pause too. He wasn't the altruistic type. And that was being generous. On the other hand, Izzy was definitely right about the need for change in fairy politics. The fairies would never truly be free until they made their own decisions, good or bad. I wanted to say as much, but Grumpy was already moving on.

"Isabella is responsible for what comes next," he said, slamming his highball glass on the bar. Brown liquor splashed up, running over the lacquered wood. Like a pro, the bartender mopped up the spill without interrupting us.

I grabbed the glass from Grumpy's hand, downing what was left of the forty-year-old scotch in a single gulp. When the burn of the alcohol curled through my bloodstream, I said, "Izzy only has the fairies' best interest at heart. She wants to help—"

"Ha!" He slapped the bar, rattling my glass as well as the nerves of the overworked bartender. "You know nothing. Your precious Isabella wants to destroy us, to take revenge for the slight she felt after her father Arnold's death." He stopped, his eyes searching my face. "She will destroy you too, and soon. From what I understand the wheels are already in motion."

I frowned. "What's that supposed to mean?"

"How much do you know about your new employee?" Grumpy asked with an evil smirk, a grin that suited him well. The bastard just oozed malice. A shiver of electricity sparked inside me at his warning. Izzy wasn't out to get me. At least I thought she wasn't. Then again, last year I'd thought the same thing and had nearly died because of it.

Not liking where this conversation or my mind was going, I growled, "Get to the point."

"Boyer & Davis," he said with relish, "has a nice ring to it, doesn't it?" No fucking way. After all we built together, Izzy wasn't going to suddenly toss me out. My expression must've betrayed my thoughts, because Grumpy's smile widened. "A guy like you must be careful around electricity."

Now I knew Grumpy was full of shit. Izzy had nothing to do with either James's murder or my attempted one as he was implying. I didn't know who exactly wanted me dead quite yet, but the list of suspects, though fairly long, didn't include anyone with pink wings. I started to say as much, but the geezer cut me off. "Mark my words."

With those dire words in the air between us, he motioned for another drink. I let out a sigh of relief. Grumpy was an angry drunkard and nothing more. The Fairy Council hadn't sent him here to hurt

Izzy, at least not physically. As for his warning about Izzy and Clark, it was complete bollocks. I hopped off the stool, giving Grumpy a pat on the shoulder with my gloved hand. "Enjoy the party," I said, unable to help myself.

He snorted. "Thank you, I will." He paused, his watery eyes blazing. "And you be sure to give James my best when you see him again."

CHAPTER 20

James's charred corpse flickered through my vision and my stomach clenched, sending a wave of alcohol-infused bile up the back of my throat. Had Grumpy just threatened me? Again? Trying to control my own anger before I did something rash, like electrocute the head of the Fairy Council in front of a couple of hundred witnesses including the chief of the New Never City Police, I walked slowly away from the bitter council member. I could feel his evil stare on my back.

Maybe Grumpy wasn't as harmless as I'd thought.

"He's a very dangerous dwarf," Right said.

I gave a small jump when he spoke, unaware that he and his book-end partner had been following me. "Damn it. I could've fried you. Next time give me a little warning."

One of his eyebrows rose. "We've been ten steps behind you all night."

In my defense, I'd been a wee bit distracted by the curves of Izzy's dress and my own growing sense of impending doom. "Well, knock it off. Izzy's the one in danger tonight. If anything happens to her, I'm kicking both your asses." And with that warning, I headed back to the ballroom where Clayton held court. I watched as he made the rounds, shaking hands and smiling with all thirty-four of his teeth (he'd had two implanted right after the primaries). "Give the fairies what they want" was his motto.

Which made me wonder, was one of those things me roasting on a spit? After all, the fairies would've liked nothing more than to see me dead. Had Clayton gone as far as attempting my murder to win the election? I shook my head at the thought, feeling more and more like the famed, paranoid recluse Humpty Hughes without the germ phobia or the bankroll.

A husky, drawn-out laugh caught my attention. I turned to the delightful sound, feeling instantly better. Izzy stood surrounded by winged and nonwinged dignitaries, a smile on her lips. She let out another chuckle at something Clark said. In a flash, whatever pleasure I'd felt from Izzy's laughter withered. Apparently, on top of being a social media guru, Clark was a fucking comedian to boot.

My lips curved into a deep frown all but guaranteed to leave me looking worse than Grumpy in ten years. A small hand pulled on the sleeve of my jacket. I glared down at the offending limb, then remembered my promise to Izzy to try to be nice. I turned my frown halfway upside down, the best I could do at the moment, leaving my lips a flat line.

"Blue," Peyton said, pulling at my sleeve again, this time with much greater force.

"What?" I snapped.

He dropped my sleeve, stepping back. "I'm . . . ah . . . glad you're here."

At least someone was.

Personally I would rather be at a dark bar drowning in a barrel of aged whiskey. My gaze again fell upon Izzy. This time Clark had his hand wrapped around her like Velcro. Make that two barrels. My frown returned. Peyton must've sensed my displeasure, for he looked around until his eyes lit on Izzy and Clark. "They make a cute couple." He beamed with pride and pleasure. "Don't you think?"

"What the fuck do you want, Peyton?"

His head moved back and forth as he made tsking sounds. "No need to be like that. Clark's a good man. The Boyers are old money. Very old. Very rich. So no need to worry that he's some gold digger trying to get his hooks into Isabella. You can relax."

"Excuse me?"

"We know how you feel. But you don't need to be so protective of Izzy anymore." He nodded to the pink wings in question. "Clark can take care of her, and you can get on with your life." His grin grew as Clark leaned down to whisper in her ear.

I bit my tongue, drawing blood.

"Clayton and I knew they'd hit it off the moment we met Clark."

And why not? Clark didn't have electrical issues. He was rich and good-looking, the perfect fucking catch for Izzy. Except I had my doubts Izzy was looking to be caught in anyone's net. She was much more likely to be the one setting a trap. I just hoped it wasn't the one Grumpy had insinuated.

Peyton was saying, "I'd be surprised if Izzy isn't married and pregnant by this time next year."

My blood pressure rose at the thought of Clark's baby in Izzy's wings. Electricity crackled inside me, escaping from my ungloved hand. Peyton yelped as he danced from the errant bolt. "Hey—" he complained.

I winced. "Sorry."

"What's going on with you?" His eyes narrowed, his head swiveling to the right and then the left as if someone might jump out at any moment. "Is it the case?"

"Case?"

"Our case." He frowned. "The missing—"

I slapped my hand, the one with the glove, over his mouth. "We're keeping the case on the DL, remember?"

He nodded and I moved my hand away. "Have you learned anything?"

"I have a few leads." All of which were crap. I was no closer to solving the missing-fairy case than I was to finding James's killer or walking on the moon. But I wasn't about to share my failures with Peyton. For one thing, he'd revel in them. While he wanted me to find out what had happened to the fairies, he sure as hell wouldn't shed a tear if I failed and/or ended up a broken pile of blue-haired goo. Neither of those options appealed to me. I would solve both cases or die trying, which didn't appeal very much to me either.

"Maybe Clark can help—" The electrical shock I shot at him this time wasn't an accident. His eyes rolled like pinwheels for a brief moment as the bolt jolted through him and then returned to their normal state. "Or not," he finished in a high-pitched squeak. "Now that I think about it, it's probably best if we keep it to ourselves."

"You're probably right."

A fork dinged against a crystal glass, signaling the stump speeches were about to begin. Shoot me now, I thought, and then Izzy giggled at Clark again. And I thought, Nope, shoot him. Please.

CHAPTER 21

Much to my dismay, Izzy and I were seated at the head table next to Clayton and Peyton. The twins had also asked Clark to sit at our table, on Izzy's other side. The salad course arrived and Clark made a joke about accidently biting Clayton's emerald-colored wing. The entire table laughed, with one exception. Yours bluely. I wasn't sure I could make it through the entrée before frying the VP. I took a deep breath, digging into my wilted salad before I acted on the impulse.

Halfway through the dinner, Izzy squeezed my leg under the table as if she recognized Clark's peril. She leaned in, whispering, "Thank you, Blue."

I glanced up from my plate, my forehead wrinkled in question. "For what?"

She motioned around the crowded ballroom. "For putting up with all of this."

"Come on," I said with a quick grin, "I'm having the time of my life."

Her eyes flashed with mirth. "I can tell."

"How so?"

She jabbed the thrice-electrocuted piece of now blackened chicken on my plate. "A woman always knows."

"Is that so?"

She grinned. "And you've been vibrating like crazy for the last twenty minutes."

I took a calming breath. "Sorry."

"Is something bothering you besides the fire in your office?"

Hell, the fire had been the last thing on my mind. Too many other things took precedence, namely, keeping Izzy safe while finding out who killed my intern. I wanted to talk to Izzy about the murder and Grumpy's warning. "Izzy, we need to—"

"And now for the fairy of the hour . . ." The crowd quieted. "Please welcome the next Tooth Fairy . . . Clayton Gibbs." Applause filled the ballroom, drowning out my words. Izzy leaned in closer, but I waved her off with a "later" gesture. She nodded and gave me a small yet concerned smile.

Clayton puffed out his tiny chest as he took the stage. I had to admit, he looked very toothy in his tuxedo, dyed wings, and dust-infused swagger. Hell, if I didn't know him so well I might've even voted for him. Good thing I didn't have wings. No wings, no vote, which I was cool with.

"Thank you all for being here," he began, "And for your support. We all know the difficult times we face . . ."

I grinned. Half those difficult times were a direct result of Clayton's actions.

"I want you to know that I understand . . ."

I tuned out, watching the expressions of those in the crowd. Most of the winged ones were hanging on his every word, their eyes alight with promise. Those without wings listened too, but with less enthusiasm and more self-interest. Sadly, not everyone fell into that category. Clark, it seemed, only had eyes for Izzy. It was creepy. Every time I glanced over at the guy, he was looking our way, eyes burning with desire. I glared at him until he snapped out of it. He responded with a guilty smile.

"Crime is up . . . ," Clayton was saying.

I rolled my eyes; pretty damn sure the crime rate, like those difficulties he'd referred to earlier, was, at least partially, the twins' fault. Hell, I'd committed more than one crime while in their company and their employ. That was in the past, though—the not-too-distant one, but history nonetheless. My focus returned to Clayton's speech.

"But I have a plan." He paused, his gaze falling on Izzy's face. A shiver of dread curled up my spine. "Our beloved Isabella Davis's company, Davis Securities, has been hired to solve the crime of the century."

Davis Securities? What the hell? Clayton had just cut me out of my own company. I blew out a harsh breath. I knew why he'd done it. The fairies hated me with a fiery passion, but they adored Izzy.

Therefore, Reynolds & Davis became strictly Davis. I glanced over at Izzy to see how she'd responded, but all I saw was shock and rage in her indigo eyes.

I frowned. "What?"

"You took the case without consulting me?" she hissed under her breath. "How could you?" At this point I wasn't sure what case she was talking about. After all, I'd taken any number of cases without a powwow. Then Clayton's speech finally penetrated my brain.

"The missing fairies are Davis Securities' and my own top propriety." Clayton paused while the crowd applauded. "We will find the person or persons responsible and make them pay. You have my word on it."

The little bastards had set me up. They couldn't care less about a gaggle of missing fairies; they only wanted to seem like they gave a shit. With Izzy on the case, Clayton was all but guaranteed to win the election. "Izzy," I began, but it was too late.

My pink-winged fairy had left the ball.

Not a glass slipper left in sight.

CHAPTER 22

After dinner I searched everywhere for Izzy, but she'd vanished, as had Clark Boyer. That bit of information gnawed its way into my brain, making rational thought impossible. Izzy was a grown woman, I reminded myself again and again. Free to do what and *whom* she pleased, generally with the exception of our employees. I wrapped myself in self-righteous rage instead of the vague sense of guilt I felt in not telling Izzy about the missing-fairies case.

Lucky for me, anger was my go-to emotion. I often thrived on rage, the kind that burned just below the surface. The nuns claimed my temper and subsequent electrical conductivity were a direct result of having been abandoned as a baby.

I knew better.

I was born a monster.

My mind flashed to Izzy lying naked in Clark's stupid arms as energy crackled through me in electrified waves. How dare she sleep with him? He could sue us for sexual harassment, and then where would we be? Bad enough James had died in the line of duty; now we had to worry about opening ourselves up to Clark's greed.

My anger followed me all the way back to my apartment. I vowed to have it out with Izzy. She would probably break down, begging my forgiveness and firing Clark instantly. I smiled at my deluded fantasy as I unlocked my front door.

As soon as I took my first step inside, a ruby slipper came flying my way. It barely missed my head, smashing into the door behind me with a muffled thud. "Whoa," I yelled, holding up my hands. "What the hell, Izzy?"

"Are you kidding me?" My partner in crime solving let the second slipper fly. My catlike reflexes saved me from a nasty lump as I ducked out of the projectile's way just in time. "Do you have any idea how pissed I am at you?"

From the flying slippers and the heaving of her barely contained breasts, I had a pretty fair idea. "So I took a case." I shook my head, going on the defensive. "What's the big deal? We are investigators. Investigating cases is sort of what we do. I've taken plenty of cases without a lengthy discussion. What makes this one any different?"

My reasoning didn't cool her rage one bit. In fact, it seemed to enrage her even more. Her eyes flashed with blue flames. "You purposely kept *this* case a secret from me. A fairy case from your fairy partner." Her shoulders slumped. "I thought we were past this. Past keeping secrets and lying to each other."

Guilt pooled in my gut along with the rubbery overcooked chicken from dinner. I swallowed, pushing both further down. "Izzy. I didn't mean to—"

"Lie to me?" She snorted. "Or you didn't mean for me to find out?"

"The second one," I admitted. "I didn't want you involved."

She took a step toward me. "So you were protecting me?"

The soft way she asked the question was all the warning I needed. "Hell no. You are more than capable of protecting yourself. I was . . . um . . ."

"What you are is an idiot."

I ignored her insult, preparing myself to ask the question that had been burning in my mind. The one Grumpy had instilled and later Clayton and his Davis Securities comment had cemented. Did Izzy want me out? As much as I wanted that answer, my tongue had other plans. "What's with you and Clark?"

"What?"

"Are you dating him?" This time I wanted to bite off my treacherous tongue. What was wrong with me? What she did after hours was none of my business. I felt like a stupid schoolboy with a secret, obsessive crush on the head cheerleader. A cheerleader with wings and a hell of a right hook, I reminded myself, stepping out of striking distance.

She crossed her arms over her chest, a clear indication she was about to let me have it. "You're kidding, right? Less than six hours ago I walked in on you and your little friend Bo Peep, and I didn't say a fucking word about how incredibly stupid you are for getting involved with the likes of her. And now you have the audacity to ask me about Clark?"

While she had a point, I wasn't quite willing to let it go, which only proved her assessment of my intelligence all the more. "Nothing happened with Bo. I thought she had—"

"Oh," she said. "I know exactly what you thought she had for you."

"Hey," I complained.

She waved me off. "If we're going to stay partners, we need complete and total honesty between us."

I nodded slowly, wondering just where she planned to go with this.

Her eyebrows rose. "Well?"

"Well what?"

She rolled her indigo-colored irises. "Tell me about the case."

"No."

"What?" Her screech nearly knocked her off her bare feet.

I moved around her, keeping at least three feet of distance between us. I picked up a bottle of whiskey from the coffee table, pouring a shot into a glass tumbler. I waved it her way. She shook her head, her face growing redder by the second. "We do need to talk, but not about the missing-fairy case," I said quietly.

Her expression turned from annoyed to suspicious. "About what, then? If you say Clark, I'm leaving right now."

"I'm not talking about Clark." Not exactly. I swallowed my whiskey in one gulp, letting the burn of it ease the taste of my next words. My eyes met hers, and Grumpy's warning flickered through my mind again. "Do you have something to tell me, Izzy?" I asked, my voice barely above a whisper.

Seconds passed in silence.

Finally she slowly turned her back to me. "How'd you find out?"

"It's kind of what I do." For better or worse. Her reaction to the question told me everything I needed to know. Grumpy wasn't lying. She planned to oust me from my own company. Anger swept through me, sending a current of electricity so strong up my spine that my hair stood on end. "Is it true? Are you—"

"Yes," she said sharply. "But you weren't supposed to find out."

I laughed without humor. "You are in cahoots with Clark to take over my co—"

"Wait! What?" she yelled, spinning to face me, her hands flying to her hips. "You think I'm involved in a takeover? Are you nuts?"

My eyes narrowed. "Are you saying you're not?"

"Of course not." She laughed with bitterness. "I'm not like your flea-riddled girlfriend—"

"Forget Bo Peep," I said, reaching for her arm. My fingers closed around her forearm, generating a slight spark. I quickly dropped it before I hurt her. "If you're not involved in a hostile takeover, what the hell have you been keeping from me?"

She winced. "Why don't you take a seat . . ."

CHAPTER 23

"You're working a case without telling me?" I shook my head for the tenth time since she'd spilled her proverbial beans. I couldn't believe her. She'd been working some case for more than a month without my knowledge. I pictured the danger she could face while on a case, any case, and the lowlifes who would cut out her heart for a few bucks. I wanted to shake her until her very strong white teeth rattled.

One of her flame-colored eyebrows rose. "And this is different from you taking Peyton's missing-fairy case how?"

"Because . . . I . . . ah . . ." I jumped from the couch to pace. "It just is, damn it." I jabbed my finger at her. "I'm the investigator. You are . . ."

"I'm what, Blue?" she asked in a dangerous tone. "A pretty face? A trophy partner? How exactly do you see our working relationship?"

I shook my head. "You're putting words in my mouth. I just meant, I have experience working cases."

"And I don't?" She shook her head. "I remember solving my fair share over the last year."

"Together," I said. "*We* solved those cases. Not you by yourself." I rushed on before she could argue. "Investigations can be very dangerous, Izzy. People can get hurt." I paused, pushing my next words through the lump in my throat at the very thought of any harm coming to her. "You could get hurt."

For a moment, the anger left her face and she looked resigned. "I won't."

"You don't know that." I licked my dry lips. "Please, let me help you. We can work the case together, whatever it might be. I'll even let you take the lead."

"Let me?" She snorted, her voice rising with each word. "You'll let me take the lead on my own case?"

I held up my hand. "Take it easy. I'm merely trying to help."

"Then keep your mouth shut." She poked her finger into my chest. Hard. A blue bolt of electricity shot from me to her finger, but she didn't seem to notice the electrical charge. "You go ahead and work your missing-fairy case, and I'll work mine. When it's over"—her eyes met mine and her voice quieted—"we will reevaluate."

"Reevaluate what, Izzy?" I asked, though I had a damn good idea what she wanted to reassess.

"Us."

Following her proclamation, Izzy walked out of my apartment, closing the door quietly behind her. I stared at the closed door, a feeling of imminent doom sweeping through me. I was a fool. Izzy had talked me in circles, avoiding spilling any of her secrets, and now I was left staring at a closed door, wondering what kind of case she was working and whether or not she was sleeping with Clark. My fists clenched, and I considered chasing after her.

But I'd lost my chance.

Before I took a step toward the door, it flew open, smacking against the wall with a loud bang. Izzy stormed back inside, her eyes burning violet. "Damn it, Blue. You can't leave your door unlocked so just anyone can bust inside and kill you. Do you not remember James lying dead on the floor?"

"I—"

Her finger wagged in my direction. "I don't want to hear any excuses. Just lock your door."

"Okay," I agreed, which drained all of her righteous anger.

She sighed deeply. "All right, then."

"Is that why you came back?" I took a cautious stride closer to her, until we were less than a foot apart. "To make sure I lock my door?"

"Of course." Her tongue darted out, wetting her lips. "What other reason would I have?"

We stood there, silence growing between us.

Finally Izzy gave me a small, sad smile. "Right and Left are standing guard in the hall. Try not to get yourself killed before morning."

CHAPTER 24

The next morning I dressed in a pair of jeans and a sweatshirt, poured a cup of three-day-old coffee into a chipped mug, and plopped down on my couch to contemplate my next move. It had been three days since I'd found James dead on my floor. One day since Izzy had walked in on me and Bo Peep. And less than eight hours since she'd walked out my door with her secrets intact. Suffice it to say, I hadn't gotten much sleep.

I rubbed my eyes, downing half the cup of coffee. It tasted much worse after the third day. But caffeine didn't care if it tasted like dirt; it worked miracles no matter what. My heart started to beat with pleasure and an electrical pulse. Taking a deep breath, I picked up my cell phone from the coffee table and punched in a phone number from memory.

Bad memories, to be precise.

Memories better left in the past.

But I had no choice if I wanted to find James's killer.

"Locks," the detective answered on the third ring, sounding much worse than I felt.

"Good morning, Detective," I said in my sincerest voice. "Hope I didn't wake you."

"Who is this?" she asked in a hoarse whisper.

"Blue Reynolds."

"How did you get my cell number?" Her voice grew stronger with each word, until my phone crackled with anger. Lucky for me, Detective Goldie Locks couldn't shoot people through the phone. I bet she wished for such a power right now.

Rather than answer that loaded question about the means by which

I'd obtained her mobile number, all of which were very illegal, I said, "I know that you're a busy woman so I'll be quick—"

"Too late."

I ignored her statement. "I was calling to see if you've made any headway on the Wild case."

Silence greeted my inquiry.

"Locks?" I asked after thirty seconds of nothingness. "You still there?"

"Yeah," she answered. "Mr. Reynolds, I promise that as soon as we have a suspect, you'll be the first to know. Now, if you'll excuse me—"

"Detective," I said sharply.

She blew out a drawn-out sigh. "Look," she said, "we're doing all we can, but you have to understand—"

"Oh, I understand perfectly." I gripped the phone tighter, my fingers smoldering against the plastic. "A charbroiled intern isn't top priority. Not in a city this size. At least not to the NNPD." I paused, letting my words sink in. "But it is to me. Either you do your damn job, or else . . ."

"Is that a threat?"

"No, Detective. It's a promise."

Following my call to Detective Locks, I pulled on my leather jacket and a pair of thick gloves and then headed for my front door. I wasn't lying to the good detective. I would find James's killer with or without the NNPD's help.

A few minutes later I left my apartment and jumped on the Fey Train uptown to the offices of Reynolds & Davis Securities. When I arrived at the office it appeared deserted, with the exception of Izzy's bitchy administrative assistant seated primly at her desk, filing her talon-like nails to even finer points. All the better to stab anyone without an appointment.

"Ms. Davis isn't in," she sneered when she finally bothered to glance my way. "She called to say she had a late night and wouldn't be in until later. I heard a man in the background. He sounded hot . . . Now that I think about it, Mr. Boyer hasn't arrived yet either . . ."

I ignored her and turned down the hall toward my fire-damaged office. The closer I got, the greater the acrid stench of smoke. My eyes started to water when I opened the door. My mouth dropped open and I took a step back, surveying the destruction in front of me.

Half of the office was completely destroyed, from my old, worn desk to the file cabinets against the far wall. The other half appeared untouched by the flames, as if someone had drawn a line from one side to the other. Of course, everything not burned to a crisp was completely soaked in water and fire retardant. My feet squished on the carpet as I entered the room.

Good thing I'd worn rubber-soled shoes.

I winced, noticing for the first time that the expensive artwork Izzy had meticulously picked out just for me, mostly from Picasso's Blue Period, was charred at the edges. I moved toward my desk, my chest aching with every step as I tore off my gloves. Large black scorch marks raced across the desktop. My laptop lay in a puddle, thoroughly melted from the flames, as if it was ground zero. Licking my dry lips, I reached down to pull out what used to be the bottom drawer of my desk. It slid forward an inch and then disintegrated in my hands.

I closed my eyes, fearing the worst.

I wasn't disappointed.

The file, my file, lay in a pile of ash.

Gone. It was all gone. What I knew of my early life, had collected meticulously for years, was now dust and ash. Burned up in an instant.

Anger swept through me, quick and hot, much like the fire itself. My fingers brushed the charred remnants of my life. Hell, it wasn't like I could burn them even more. I glanced around the office, resigning myself to the truth. Like James's murder, this wasn't an accident. Someone had torched my office on purpose, using a fast-burning accelerant. Alcohol maybe. I looked on the floor, not too surprised to see a bottle of expensive whiskey, the same brand I kept in the bottom drawer with the file, lying in the ash. The bottle was empty.

The fire was a spur-of-the-moment crime.

Not a well-executed crime either. Quick and dirty.

But effective.

Why? What did someone gain by destroying my office?

Izzy knocked on the open door, gasping in shock when she saw the damage. It took every ounce of willpower I had not to question her about her late night or whom she'd been with. My fingers dug into my palms, leaving tiny half-moon indents on my flesh.

Izzy waved a hand in front of her face as she entered the destruction. "Reminds me of the last time we went to happy hour."

I couldn't help but laugh. The tension in my muscles eased a bit. "I did pay for the damages."

"Of course, you could've avoided the whole debacle if you'd just let Clayton win."

"He was cheating." I frowned, growing annoyed all over again. "At bar trivia. Who does that?"

Her lips curved into a wicked smile as she raised a guilty hand. "I was, but you didn't electrify my barstool."

My annoyance vanished under her obvious humor. I lifted my shoulder in a shrug, feeling better than I had all morning. "But you're just a girl. You have to cheat in order to win."

Her small fist came out of nowhere, smacking me in the arm with enough force to leave a mark. Luckily the resulting shock did nothing more than bring a frown to her lips as she blew on her fist. "Hey," I complained. "I should file a complaint with HR. Workplace violence is the number one killer of—"

"Complaint denied."

I grinned. "So soon?"

She shrugged. "What can I say? I'm efficient."

"You, my winged partner, are many things . . ." I trailed off, watching her closely.

She sniffed the air. "Are you smoking again?"

I thought of the cigarette I'd enjoyed less than twenty minutes ago and shook my head. "Of course not; you know I quit six months ago."

"Are you sure?"

"Izzy, you smell the smoke from the fire. Nothing more." To take her mind off my vices, many of which I longed for right now, I motioned around the charred office. "Did the security system catch anything?"

She shook her head. "No, nothing."

"Figures," I said. After all, we'd spent more than fifty thousand dollars on the system a few months ago. It had cameras covering every single nook and cranny, not to mention motion detectors and heat sensors. Hell, the damn thing went off as soon as I got within five hundred feet of the building, and yet, somehow, it failed to notice my office turning to cinders. Convenient.

A little too much so for my peace of mind.

Though I'd sworn to tell Izzy everything from now on, I decided to break my word just this once. It was my office that had burned, after all. That and the very real possibility that whoever had set the fire had also murdered my intern and wouldn't think twice about killing another innocent victim who got in his or her way were reason enough to keep this to myself.

So many questions swirled through my mind. But one kept repeating, like a blowing horn inside my head: Had the arsonist specifically targeted the file or was this a more general warning? I suspected the latter given that most of the file was worthless, just random pieces of a puzzle I was very far from ever solving. I bit my lip, thinking about another fire—one that happened thirty-one years ago in a maternity ward at the New Never City Hospital.

Were the fires somehow connected?

I shook my head at the fanciful notion. Arsonists didn't wait thirty-one years to burn up a few pieces of yellowed paper. Something else was going on, something connected to James's death, I was fairly sure.

CHAPTER 25

More than thirty years ago a fire started in the maternity ward of the New Never City Hospital. No one knew exactly what had caused the flames to erupt. Some claimed faulty wiring while others wondered if God had passed judgment on one of the newborn souls. I suspected the latter to be true. But not just any newborn—a blue-haired one born to an unknown mother who later left said child on the doorstep of an orphanage.

Christine Connors was the nurse on duty when the fire started.

She knew what happened that night.

I could feel it in my bones.

What I couldn't do was find either hide or hair of Nurse Connors.

After that night she, too, had vanished in a whiff of smoke.

But not for long. Today would be the day I would finally find the woman I'd been looking for.

An hour later, after Izzy left me to do some work in her own office, I followed the cubicle farm to the very last desk tucked between the soda machine and the men's room. It was there I found just what I was looking for, or rather who I was looking for—Alice Glass—the best, albeit clumsiest, investigator in the city. At least the best one with boobs.

After all, I was no investigational slouch.

Izzy and I had hired Alice three months ago when Alice moved to the city from the outer borough of Queens of Hearts. At the time everyone had laughed, saying we had made a big mistake. Sure, Alice closed cases, they said, but she also had burned down two offices, broken the legs of several of her dates, and left a general swath of accidental destruction wherever she went. All valid points, we soon learned, when Alice managed to drop a computer on a very wealthy client with a gold digger for a wife.

Luckily for us, and for Alice, the client took one look into Alice's bespectacled blue eyes, dumped his gold-digging wife, and vowed to marry Alice as soon as the ink was dry on the divorce papers.

Since then Alice had proved herself a valued asset to our growing team.

As long as we didn't let her in the field or near our clients.

Not really a problem, since Alice preferred to stay tucked in her cubicle, scouring the Internet for clues. I used technology to solve cases, but I preferred the old ways, kicking ass and taking names on the mean, dirty streets, harder to do since the mayor had taken to regular street sweeping and jailing dirtbags willing to sell their own fairy godmothers. Alice, on the other hand, could learn anything about anyone with a few clicks of the keys. Less mess, and a hell of a lot less fun, but to each investigator his or her own.

I knocked on her cubicle wall. "Hey, Alice, got a second?"

She jumped out of her chair, spilling a cup of searing-hot liquid all over both of us. I stifled a yelp as sparks shot from my skin. "Oh, Blue, I mean, Mr. Reynolds, I'm so sorry." She wiped at my soaked shirt with her hand, shocking both of us with a decent amount of current.

Startled by my conductivity, she leapt back, nearly toppling her workstation. I grabbed it in time, but it was too late to save her. Alice landed hard on the ground at my feet. Her legs sprawled wide, showing off a pair of day-of-the-week panties.

Being a gentleman, I turned my head, barely noticing "Friday" embroidered up the side.

Alice managed to pull herself together, and once she settled back in her office chair, I got down to business. "Any luck on locating Christine Connors yet?" I asked. Since I'd given her the assignment only an hour ago I didn't expect much, and I was more than a little shocked when Alice's fingers flew across her keyboard, golden hair dancing with every keystroke. Images, words, and numbers flashed over the computer screen faster and faster until my stomach gurgled more from motion sickness than from the whiskey I'd consumed the night before.

Less than a minute later a photograph of an older woman in a hospital uniform appeared on the screen. "You couldn't find her because thirty years ago she changed her name to Christine Quick, erasing all traces of Christine Connors," Alice said, her head tilting to one side. She drew her bottom lip through her teeth, lost in thought. "Which couldn't have been cheap. This lady was hiding something from someone."

My throat tightened. "Was?"

Alice's fingers paused over the keys and she glanced up. Her dark-framed glasses slid down her nose, changing her whole appearance. Suddenly her gawkiness turned to Fairymate of the Year material. Odd that I hadn't noticed until that moment how beautiful Alice was with her flaxen locks, wildflower-blue eyes, and trim body. My eyes narrowed on the shimmering color of her hair. Then she pushed her glasses back in place, breaking me from my thoughts.

"When did Christine die?" My last clue to the circumstances surrounding my birth and curse was fading before my eyes. I'd always had hope that Christine Connors was the key. The disappointment at her death nearly overwhelmed me. The burned-up file had been bad enough . . . Hope that I would one day be free from this electrical curse, free to touch and be touched by another person without a tube of Neosporin handy, dried up.

With Christine dead I would never know the truth. I would never know why I was abandoned on the steps of a church, a little blue-haired baby with a shocking secret the nuns, for lack of a better name, had christened Little Boy Blue.

"Die?" Alice shook her head, her pale face glowing under the greenish office lighting. "No, you misunderstood. Christine Quick isn't dead."

The pounding in my heart eased. "Thank God. So where is she?"

Alice winced. "You're not going to like it."

CHAPTER 26

Christine Quick was currently a resident of Shady Wings Nursing Home, which was bad enough given the name of the place, but she also suffered from severe dementia, at least according to Alice, whose information was usually right.

That spark of hope I'd had when Alice had declared Christine alive started to wither and then finally died altogether when I caught a flash of wing out of the corner of my eye. Damn. I'd planned to keep Izzy as far away from my past as possible. The less she knew about my early years, the better. I pictured the smoldering remains of the orphanage and swallowed hard. One thing was for sure: No matter what I said, Izzy would meddle. It was her nature, and I'd accepted it, for the most part.

But not this time.

I thanked Alice and stalked off to find my eavesdropping fairy. I located her about ten feet from her office. "Isabella," I said in greeting.

"Oh, Blue," she said with an innocent smile as she spun to face me, her eyes wide with affected virtuousness, "you scared me half to death."

"Uh-huh."

Her smile grew wider until it looked like her face might crack. "Was there something you needed?"

I snorted at the loaded question. "How about a partner who doesn't listen in on private conversations?"

"What?' With an indignant gasp she straightened to her full five-foot-three height. "I would never . . ."

"Right," I said with a shake of my head, ignoring her obvious attempts to gain the upper hand. "Then you didn't hear me ask Alice to do the humpty-dumpty right there on her desk?"

She rolled her eyes. "Do I look stupid enough to fall for that pathetic attempt to get me to admit I was eavesdropping? Frankly I'm embarrassed for you."

I let out a loud bark of laughter. The bitchy receptionist glanced up from her manicure with disgust. I disregarded her, focusing instead on my partner. "So you admit nothing?"

She shrugged, her wings rising and falling with guiltlessness. "How about this? I'll admit to listening in on your not-so-private conversation if you take me with you to talk to Christine Quick. It's really a win-win for both of us."

"No."

"Come on, Blue. This is important to you."

"Yes," I said. "*To me*. Not to a nosy fairy with a business to run. Think of what would happen if you weren't around to keep us afloat. Our employees count on you for direction. I count on you."

She sighed. "True."

"All right, then." I smiled. "I'll call you if anything comes up."

She tucked her arms under her breasts in an attempt to either distract or influence me. I wasn't sure which. Not that it mattered in the least. I enjoyed the view nonetheless. "Then you're excited to go into Fairyland for the second time in two days, this time to talk to an old woman with dementia who lives in a nursing home? A nursing home filled with old people who smell like death and mothballs? Not to mention, an entire winged staff who most likely want to see you run down by a passing pumpkin coach?" She looked down at her manicure, running her finger over each nail in a slow, deliberate manner. "Sounds like fun. I guess I'll leave you to it."

And as easy as that, I lost the argument and gained a nosy travel companion. I blew out a loud, annoyed sigh. "We leave in ten minutes. If you're not downstairs and ready to go, I'm leaving without you."

She laughed. "Yeah, right."

Twenty minutes later I glared at my watch for the fourth time. Izzy was late, as usual, and I was waiting, as usual. I considered the ramifications of lighting up a cigarette and then thought better of it. Izzy and I were on thin ice as it was. Add in my lying to her about quitting—again—and I would never hear the end of it.

No sooner had I decided against lighting up than Izzy pushed through the glass-and-chrome front doors. The doorman tried to open them for her, but she was much quicker with her wings than she looked. When she pulled to a stop in front of me I motioned to my watch, a watch she'd bought me on our company's one-month anniversary, saying something snarky about my work habits. Too bad for her the watch rarely kept the right time, probably a result of the electrical field around me. Though I still wore the watch every day, a silly reminder of what we'd accomplished so far.

"You said twenty minutes, right?" she asked with complete sincerity.

I shook my head and waved to a passing taxi.

It failed to stop.

I tried again.

Same result.

Eight tries later, Izzy stepped in front of me, pulled down her camisole a half an inch, and then waved one slender arm in the air. A yellow cab steered across three lanes of traffic, screeching to a stop at the curb in front of us, nearly causing a four-car pileup. Car horns blared in response, deafening me and everyone else in a block radius.

I rolled my eyes and motioned Izzy inside, and together, much against my better judgment, we set off to Fairyland to find Christine Quick. And fast.

CHAPTER 27

The Shady Wings Nursing Home wasn't in a shady part of town; it was in *the* shady part. Hard to imagine, since all of Fairyland was less than respectable. The building itself was redbrick, the sidewalk lined with drooping flowers and wilted residents. Not the most welcoming of sights. I worried about what condition we'd find Christine Quick in. Would she be lucid or a vegetable like her bathrobe-wearing compatriots? Considering my luck, she'd probably died ten minutes ago. I shook off the dire thought.

I held the door open for Izzy, motioning for her to enter. Not that I was a gentleman or thought Izzy was incapable of opening the door for herself. I was just stalling, bolstering up the courage to face whatever lay beyond the grey intuitional painted hallway. The secrets of my birth and subsequently my curse might be within reach for the first time in my life. For a moment I froze, and then Izzy touched my sleeve, and the thrall that held me vanished.

I was ready to meet my electric destiny.

"Can I help you?" a polite fairy with her hair tied back in a tight bun and thick-framed glasses asked, glancing up from behind a worn reception desk. The way she asked the question made me think visitors, winged and nonwinged alike, weren't a regular occurrence at Shady Wings.

Izzy gave her a warm smile. "Hi, I'm—"

"Your Highness," the fairy said, jumping to her tiny feet wrapped in black Mary Janes. "I'm so sorry. I didn't recognize you at first . . ."

I rolled my eyes, tired of the bowing and scraping every time Izzy walked into Fairyland. But Izzy, gracious to a fault, took the receptionist's hand in both of hers. "Please, call me Izzy."

"Really?" the fairy gushed. "I . . . I can't believe it's you . . ."

"Enough," I barked, causing a bolt of electrical current to shoot from my finger into the peeling linoleum floor. It peeled back and started to smoke. I quickly stepped on the smoldering pieces, my gaze never leaving the receptionist's shocked face. "Christine Quick. What room is she in?"

Izzy glared at me when the receptionist jumped and then turned to face the younger fairy. "I apologize for my . . . friend. Old people make him nervous."

I snorted. Fairies, not the elderly, bugged me. But I didn't correct Izzy. Not that my saying a word would have an effect anyway. She was too busy being fawned over by the growing gang of winged groupies now circling us. Some wore white coats while others wore scrubs, and even a few wore only drooping adult diapers. Not a pleasant sight. "Izzy," I said in warning.

She nodded. "We're in a bit of a hurry, so if you don't mind . . ."

The fairy receptionist jumped to attention. "Of course, Your Toothiness. Right this way." She motioned down the corridor to another hallway, where a large steel door with a glass window stood. A locked door. One meant to keep the residents inside.

But it also kept strangers out.

And Izzy and I, a half fairy and a thug, were a hell of a lot stranger than most.

"Mrs. Quick is one of our secure residents. We can't be too careful with the patients' safety," the fairy receptionist said by way of apology when we were stopped outside the locked door by an orderly who was as wide as he was tall. Not so hard to do when one was only three feet tall.

"You'll need to sign in," the orderly said to me in a gruff tone as he nodded to a metal clipboard in Izzy's hands. She was already signing her name in a flowery script. I half expected her to dot her *i*'s with tiny winged hearts. When she finished she started to hand the clipboard to me, then must've thought better of it, for she signed my name too. I frowned, saddened by the fact that I wouldn't be electrocuting the orderly with his own clipboard anytime soon.

Izzy sighed. "I can't take you anywhere."

"At least I'm consistent."

She rolled her eyes, following the orderly through the now open door and down the hall. I walked slowly behind. An old man with lizard-like skin steered himself in my path, the wheels of his chair squeaking with each rotation. I stopped abruptly before I ran him over. He mumbled something I didn't quite understand, which apparently annoyed him, for he smacked me in the knees with the cane in his lap.

"Ow," I complained, rubbing away the stinging in my bones. "What the hell?"

He smiled, showing off his empty white gums. "Can't trust the lot of them."

"Who?"

Rather than answer, he started to cackle in a loud manner. The laugh quickly turned into a horrifying cough. Green stuff flew from his lips, splattering my boots. I winced but didn't move away. Mostly because I feared he'd retaliate with a cane to my balls. Why give the geezer a better shot?

When the old guy's face turned the same shade of blue as the hair on said balls, I yelled for a nurse. No one came. I yelled louder, wondering where Izzy and the orderly had disappeared to. My second bellow received the attention the old man needed, though. A woman dressed in a white lab coat, her hair as white as three-day-old snow, ran to the wheelchair and slapped the wrinkled geezer on the back with a loud thwack, dislodging a gruesome ball of old-man goo. The goo landed an inch from my boot with a wet splat. I swear I saw the damn thing twitch.

The old guy turned to glare at me, wagged his finger, and then wheeled away, no worse for wear. I couldn't say the same. My knee still ached and I was pretty sure I now had TB or some other geezer disease. I wondered if Izzy would put me in a home.

Hopefully not this one.

"Thanks," I said to the nurse, who stood staring at me as if I'd electrocuted her best friend. Her eyes, sort of a milky blue in color, widened.

"It's you," she said. "You've come."

I frowned. "Excuse me?"

"I knew you'd come back. You and your pretty lady."

"I don't think we've met," I said, damn sure I'd remember if we had. It wasn't too often in my line of work you met a woman as old as dirt. Dirtbags rarely lived that long. "You're not a nurse, are you?" I tilted my head, staring at her for a long minute.

A wrinkle appeared between her brows on her already craggy forehead. "Am I?"

"I don't know."

The wrinkle disappeared and she smiled. "Have you seen my bedroom?"

Since I doubted she was hitting on me, I slowly shook my head. "Do you want me to?"

"That's why you're here, isn't it?"

Not that I was aware of, but who was I to argue with crazy? Hell, crazy often gave me my best clues. I motioned her forward. "After you, ma'am."

"Call me Christine."

CHAPTER 28

I couldn't believe my luck. Christine Connors Quick was standing right in front of me and appeared fairly lucid to boot. "Fairly" being a relative term. Maybe I would get some of the answers about my past after all. That thought stayed with me until we reached her room. Then my hopes faded once again. Post-it notes filled every surface of the room, decorating it like a fluorescent memory rainbow. Each sticky note offered some tiny reminder or memory. I pulled off the one on the door, which said, "The knob turns to the right."

Damn.

I felt instantly guilty for my annoyance. Yeah, I might've lost a useful clue to who I was, but Christine Connors had lost much, much more. I licked my dry lips. "Ms. Connors," I said to gain her attention, which was currently fixed on a yellow sticky note. She glanced up, her eyes seeming to focus for the briefest of seconds.

"You know who I am?" she asked in a small voice.

I nodded. "You were a nurse at the New Never City Hospital thirty years ago."

"Yes."

"There was a fire . . ."

She shook her head.

I nodded. "Yes, there was. In the maternity ward."

She shook her head harder.

"The same night a baby was born." I paused, my eyes conveying just how much I needed for her to remember. "I need to know what happened."

Her own eyes grew misty, turning them even milkier. I shifted uncomfortably, but she didn't seem to notice, too lost in her memories.

"Babies often make a relationship stronger," she said after a few moments of silence.

I nodded. Not that I had a clue about anything baby related. Thankfully, in my reckless youth, my little blue swimmers had never reached their intended destination. That I knew of. If I did have any little blue-haired kids out there, it was a shock to me, and probably a hell of one for the poor woman who had to push out a lightning rod from her vagina. "Do you remember the baby born that night?" I asked with hope. "Or the name of the couple, by any chance?"

"They loved each other more than most. Like soul mates," she said, a small smile on her face. "You could see it in their eyes."

My own eyes filled with moisture, which I quickly blinked away. Mostly for fear I'd electrocute myself. I'd always thought my parents, whoever they were, had left me on the steps of the orphanage because they hadn't been in love. That I'd been a mistake. A horrible, terrible monster made by two consenting adults. If what she said was true, my parents had abandoned me for a far different issue.

An electrical issue.

A part of me wanted to stop Christine from revealing anything more. To keep my illusions. It would be easier that way. Never knowing the truth. What was the point anyway? I would never be rid of whatever conductivity curse I possessed. This was my lot in life, I told myself. So I couldn't ever truly touch or be touched. Other people had it worse. I glanced at Christine and her mass of Post-it notes. A lot worse.

"Smith," she said.

I frowned. "Excuse me?"

"Their names—Mr. and Mrs. Smith. At least that's what they put on the birth certificate." She stopped, biting her bottom lip. "But we didn't believe them. Not really."

Damn. Another dead end. And worse, it wasn't even an original alias. No imagination, which made sense since they couldn't even leave me at a temple or, better yet, a distillery. Then again, maybe it wasn't a total loss. "Do you remember the fire? How it started?" Or better yet, who had started it?

"They loved each other more than most," she repeated. "She was so beautiful with her bright, shimmering golden hair and jade eyes. Mr. Smith was quite the looker too. All the nurses thought so. Those eyes . . . the color of the deep sea."

"The fire," I prompted when I couldn't stand to hear another word about the people who had tossed me away. "How did it start?"

She shook her head. "Fire? I don't remember a fire. Did I leave the iron on again? Some days I can't seem to remember anything . . ."

"No." I took a step toward her, my body vibrating with the need for her to remember. I took a deep, calming breath before I accidentally fried the one person who might know something about that night other than the two people who'd abandoned me. "The fire at the hospital. The Smiths had a baby and there was a fire."

Her face lifted and the years slipped away, showing off the beauty she once was before disease had stolen her mind and age ruined her body. "The baby. A baby boy."

I nodded, my throat tight. So tight I could barely push words past it. "Do you remember his name?"

"Who?"

Frustration turned my voice hoarse. "The baby's. The blue-haired baby. What was his name?"

"His name . . . It was . . . something odd . . . started with a . . ."

"What? What did it start with?" I'd never been this close to my past, to knowing who I was and where I'd come from. I was at once terrified and elated by the possibilities. "What was my name?"

"Blue," Izzy said from the doorway.

My head swiveled her way.

"Yes. Yes, that's it," Christine said.

CHAPTER 29

"Little Baby Blue," Christine said, a smile on her lips. "Mr. Smith was quite shocked to see his son had bright blue hair. I remember the look in his eyes at the odd hue; it was as if someone had put a stake through his heart." She shrugged. "Who could blame him? Neither he nor his wife had blue hair, so naturally, he must've wondered . . ."

I shook my head, suspecting poor old pops was a little more than shocked by his blue-haired offspring. At least I knew the truth now. I was born blue. This—I glanced down at my bluish arm hair—wasn't a curse given to me but some kind of birth defect. A genetic mutation. A monster made from DNA. Which meant one thing—I would never be free from it.

"But you already know this," Christine said.

I glanced up, confused.

But she wasn't looking at me. Nope, her focus was directed at the chick in the doorway. My eyes narrowed on Izzy. She shrugged, lifting her shoulders with innocence.

I motioned between Izzy and Christine. "You two know each other?"

"She's obviously confused . . ." Taking a few steps inside the room, Izzy took Christine's hand in hers, patting her yellowed and wrinkled skin. "It's okay. Tell us what you remember about Blue's birth."

"I . . . You . . . ," she murmured. "My name is Christine Quick. I was a nurse."

Izzy gave her a soft smile. "I know."

"You're a good woman," she said to the younger fairy. "And he is the right man. I can see that . . ."

I frowned. "Who?"

Izzy rolled her eyes. "She means you, you big blue idiot."

"Oh."

She snorted. "Yep, I am one hell of a lucky woman."

Christine wasn't finished with her rant. "The way he looks at you, it's like how his father looked at his mother . . ."

Izzy glanced down at her watch. "Well, would you look at the time? Blue and I have a meeting uptown, so we have to get going . . ."

My blue eyebrow rose. "We do?"

"Yes," Izzy bit out. "If you'll excuse us, Ms. Quick . . ."

"Not so fast, Isabella," I said. "Christine, what happened to me, to my parents?"

"Blue," Izzy said, her voice frosty with warning, as if she was scolding a schoolboy. A tone I'd grown used to over the last year.

But she wasn't going to win this time. I had a mission to accomplish, one I would never forget. "No," I said to Izzy, and then turned to face Christine. "She knows something about them. About me. I need to know whatever it is."

"Do I know you?" Christine looked at Izzy and then at me, her gaze as blank and unfocused as a newborn baby's.

Izzy placed her arm an inch from mine, offering comfort in her own way. I swallowed the lump in my throat and slowly nodded. Whatever secrets Christine held would stay locked inside her. At least I had a place to start.

The name Smith rang in my ears.

"No, ma'am," I said as I turned to leave. "Thank you for talking with me."

"I'm sorry," Izzy said, her hand hovering inches from mine. "I know you thought Christine would have the answers you seek."

I shook my head, staring out the grimy window of the taxi. Raindrops splashed against the glass, leaving streaks of dirt, like tears, running down the surface. "Why don't you want me to find out the truth about my past?"

"What?" Her shock sounded real enough, and it sure as hell was loud enough in the small interior of the cab. "How can you say that? I traveled across town with you today. I spent the last year following up on every tip with you." She paused, her eyes filling with tears. "I want nothing more than for you to get the closure you need. But it's time to face facts," she said quietly. "You need to stop searching for answers about your birth. The office fire was a sign. It's time to move on with your life, to let go of the past."

A sign? She thought the fire in my office was some kind of sign? I held back a laugh. If anything, the fire proved one thing: Someone was getting nervous that I was closing in on the truth. Why else burn up the only evidence surrounding the mystery of my birth?

"I'm worried about you, Blue," she said. "Your life is in danger, and yet, you don't seem to care. You're keeping secrets from me and you're using our company resources to track down ninety-year-old women."

I snorted, deflecting her argument with a pretty damn good one of my own. At least I thought so, but by the way her lips thinned I doubted she felt the same. "I'm keeping secrets? You're the one with the top secret case. Why don't you tell me what it's about, and then maybe I'll be a bit more honest myself? How's that?"

She wrapped her arms over her chest and let out a sigh. "You're deflecting again, Blue. This isn't about me. It's about you and your trust issues. If we plan to make a go of . . . our business, we need to trust each other." She stopped, her eyes hard on my face. "I need for you to stop looking into the past. Please, Blue, for us."

How I wished I could say the words she needed to hear. To tell her the past meant nothing. But it hung around me like a cloud of lightning, pulsing with the promise of violence if I let it. I vowed never to let it. A promise, like quitting smoking, I wasn't sure I could keep.

CHAPTER 30

With her words rattling around my brain, I paid the cabbie, watching as Izzy headed through the lobby of our office building. She walked with purpose, her high heels clicking against the floor in a quick rat-a-tat pattern. Everyone she passed, from the security guards to the janitor, paused to watch her walk by. It was more than just her wings; she had a presence like no other woman I'd ever met. Was that what Christine had recognized at the nursing home? Or was Izzy hiding something much darker?

I suspected the latter, which worried me. And that worried me even more. Was Izzy right? Was I projecting my own trust issues on our relationship? It wasn't like she'd given me any reason to doubt her loyalty over the last year. But before that, she had been involved in the plot to rid the fairies of yours bluely. Was Izzy once again playing me for some unforeseen reason?

Trust be damned. It was time to investigate my own partner.

I had a feeling I wasn't going to like what I found. Her closet hid some secrets—of that I had no doubts. I just hoped it wasn't full of skeletons too. Literally. I wasn't looking forward to finding yet another dead guy.

I stayed in my wet, still a bit smoky office for the rest of the afternoon looking through a few cases without much interest. Mostly fluff cases with the exception of the missing fairies. But I was no closer to finding a single missing fairy feather than I had been a few days ago when Peyton first came to me with the case. I'd called every snitch I knew, but no one had a clue as to where the fairies had gone. Frustrated, I pushed the case file to the bottom of the stack of open cases on my desk. After two hours I'd solved three of the fluff cases and was working on my fourth when my office door opened, revealing the vivacious outline of my partner. "Blue," she said quietly. "I'm heading out for the night."

"Hot date?" I joked.

Her lips lifted in the corners and her eyes twinkled. "We'll see."

My stomach plunged and my chest gave another small squeeze as I pictured her with our VP, Clark Boyer. Great, I now had stomach problems to go with my heart disease.

"I . . . I wanted to say . . . I'm sorry about earlier . . . ," she was saying.

I raised a blue eyebrow. Izzy wasn't the "I'm sorry" type. She did and said what she wanted, rarely apologizing for anything. It was one of the things I liked and hated most about her. I tilted my head to study her. "Which part?" I asked.

Her lips curved into a frown. "What do you mean?"

"Which part are you apologizing for?" I stared at her for a few seconds before continuing. "What you said? Or maybe what you haven't told me?"

Her eyebrow, this one flame colored, rose. "Are you talking about my case again?" She let out a laugh. "You just can't let it go, can you? You hate that I know something you don't. That I'm just as capable of solving cases as you are." Her laughter stilled, as did her body. "What is it? Are you afraid I'll make a go of it on my own? That you won't be able to compete?"

I snorted. "I'm far more worried that you'll end up extra-crispy like our intern. You do remember him, right?" I swallowed hard, laying my cards on the table. "There are some very bad people in this world, Izzy," I began, including myself, a mess of fairies, and probably tonight's date in the bad-people category. "People who will kill to keep their secrets. I don't want anything to happen to you. You get that, right?"

She nodded slowly. "I do. More than you know." And with that, she turned on her heel and walked from my office, closing the door quietly behind her.

I stared at the closed door for a long time after she'd gone.

CHAPTER 31

When the last Reynolds & Davis employee left for the night, including my two winged bodyguards, who were now waiting downstairs in the lobby, I stepped from my office and headed down the darkened corridor. Izzy's office was my target. Something was nagging at me about her "case." It was like a splinter sitting under my skin. I wasn't sure she was right about why I was so invested. I wasn't afraid of a little competition, as long as I came out on top. And I sure as hell wasn't worried that she was a better investigator. After all, I'd been in the game for a long time.

Unless she had help.

I pictured her and Clark, Jack and Jilling their way around the city. The thought left me cold. I shook it off as I twisted the doorknob of her office door and grinned. It was locked. Like that would keep me or really anyone with a vested interest out. I pulled a set of lock picks from my jacket and went to work. Ten seconds later the knob glided open under the pressure of my fingertips, and I pushed inside.

Izzy's office was immaculate. Not an item out of place. Her desk was as bare as Old Mother Hubbard's cupboard. No paper files in sight, which annoyed me, as I was hoping to learn all of Izzy's hidden secrets tonight. I moved across the room, settling into her office chair. The faint scent of fairy dust filled the air. I inhaled deeply, enjoying the rush of warmth through my body. Warmth I needed at the moment, because breaking and entering into my partner's office, even though I had her best interest at heart, left me cold. Don't get me wrong—I would do whatever was necessary to protect what we had.

Whatever that was.

The first thing I did after the dusty effects faded was to check her desk drawers. It was amazing what one could learn about people from the crap they kept in their desk. For instance, in my bottom desk drawer used to sit a half-empty bottle of whiskey, a handful of bullets for my .38, the file regarding my birth, and a faded picture of my younger self at the orphanage on the annual Adopt-a-Kid Day.

The hope in my gaze in the photograph had long ago faded. I was destined to walk my path alone. The kid in the photo had somewhere deep inside known that was true. Why else would I have, at the age of ten, electrocuted the one and only man and woman who'd every showed interested in adopting a blue-haired boy? I rarely thought of my time at the orphanage, and when I did, whiskey helped me to forget. But the photo was always there. A reminder of who I was. Of who I would always be.

Unless I found a way to end this curse.

I blinked a few times, letting go of the past in order to look through my partner's things. Maybe I did have a few slight trust issues, as Izzy was fond of saying. Reaching into her top drawer, I pulled out a few ounces of dentin powder in a small black vial. Dentin was the lifeblood of all fairies. Without it a fairy would last a few days, a week, tops.

I thought of the missing fairies and swallowed hard. At this point, the odds that the missing fairies were still fluttering were slim to none. Which made me that much more determined to find out who was behind their disappearances and why.

A worry for another time. I had enough on my plate already with a dead intern and an arsonist/killer on my tail. I took a deep breath and went back to the matter at hand. As long as Izzy was keeping her secret case a secret, she was in danger. And her safety was my top priority.

Full of self-righteousness, I searched through the rest of the desk drawers without much success. Though I did find a molar stained with blood, a very familiar-looking molar. Much like the one I'd had ripped out last year by a psychopath. Maybe Izzy had saved it for good luck? Or much more likely she was planning to use it in some fairy voodoo spell.

Either way, I found her keeping it sort of sweet.

I glanced at my watch—the one Izzy had given me—and then moved to her laptop computer, still docked at her station. I opened it, waiting for the screen to come to life. When it did, the username and password box appeared. Her username was easy enough—IDavis.

Now for the password. Thanks to our IT guy, the passwords changed every thirty days, so it was harder to crack than I'd first believed. I started at the top of the list of Izzy's formerly known passwords, working my way through the names of every man, woman, and winged child connected to her. Arnold hadn't worked. Neither had Clayton or Peyton. I tried her birth date. Her childhood pets' names. Her street name and zip code. And even the word "password"; given that it was the most popular password, I figured it couldn't hurt.

But I was very wrong.

The IT guy had been ready for just this sort of thing.

After my tenth try at cracking her password, the laptop froze and the screen went black. A tiny red light in the corner of her desk began to blink, alerting the building's security staff of a possible intruder. Damn it. Just what I needed. The security guards had let someone burn down my office, but let someone forget their password and all hell broke loose.

With a very quick scan of the rest of the room, I gave up my search, hightailing it back to my own office before the gun-happy cavalry arrived. Two point six minutes later, the guards arrived, guns drawn. I stepped from my office. "Everything okay?" I asked innocently.

The guards, one about six feet tall and the other half that, with wings, swung their weapons my way. I held up my arms. "Take it easy," I said in warning as electrical current rushed through me. "Jonas," I said to the smaller, winged guard, "don't even think about it."

He sighed, lowering his gun. The other guard followed suit with some reluctance. I couldn't fault the guy. It wasn't every day that a rent-a-cop got the actual chance to shoot someone. "We had an alarm," Jonas said, stepping in front of the other guard. "Someone was trying to hack Isabella's computer. Badly." He raised an eyebrow, easing some of the chubby wrinkles lining his face. "You wouldn't know anything about that, would you?"

I blinked innocently. "Of course not. Why would I hack Izzy's computer? We're equal partners. Always honest and up front with each other no matter what, just like you, Jonas."

He snorted but didn't press the issue. "So what are you doing here so late? You're usually out of here by the time happy hour starts. When you come in at all, that is."

"Working a case." I shrugged, but my eyes bore into his. "You know how it is—bad guys are all around, lying in wait, sometimes right under our noses."

He swallowed and then quickly covered his reaction with a stilted laugh. "Funny, I thought you'd gone soft and only took corporate cases now."

Electricity sparked through me, but I didn't take the bait. I wasn't a corporate PI, and I never would be. That was Izzy's thing, which got me to thinking. Whatever her secret case was, it likely had more to do with embezzlement than with murder. That had me sighing with relief.

"You can go now," I said, waving toward the elevator.

Jonas looked at the other guard and nodded once, and then they left together, but not before Jonas got the last word. "I'll be sure to mention the alarm to Isabella in the morning. I'd call her tonight, but she was going out on a date."

As the elevator doors closed, a slow smile spread across my lips, replacing the frown pulling my features down.

CHAPTER 32

I hailed a taxi twenty minutes after my encounter with Jonas, his words still whispering in my ear. When, after my tenth try, a cabbie pulled to the curb, I got in and gave him directions uptown. "There's an extra twenty in it if you lose those two." I motioned to the cab behind us, where Right and Left were climbing aboard. The cabbie nodded, slamming his foot on the gas pedal before I was even settled into my seat. As we started off I checked my pockets for the necessities: breath mints, cigarettes, gloves, cell phone, my wallet, and most important, my lock picks, for I was on a mission.

Twenty minutes later the cab stopped in front of a darkened brownstone. Izzy's brownstone, to be precise. While she was off on some date with some douche bag, hopefully not our VP, I planned on breaking into her brownstone and searching for clues. It was in her best interest, I told myself for the tenth time since the idea had popped into my head.

Yeah, I wasn't buying it either.

But I still found myself standing at her front door, lock picks in hand.

Before I broke in, I pulled a cigarette out of my pocket and lit it, watching the street for any signs of Izzy, bad guys intent on doing harm, or my fairyguards. Oddly enough, not a car passed by. It was as if the city was giving me permission to break in. I sucked in a lungful of smoke, enjoying the burning in the back of my throat nearly as much as the release of tension in my muscles. Which was why I just couldn't quit; smokes were too damn good.

With one last drag, I tapped my cigarette out on my gloved hand and stuffed the butt in my pocket. No use leaving evidence at the scene of my intended crime. With one more glance at the empty street, I broke through the lock as well as the boundaries of our relationship with ease. My hand stilled on the doorknob. This was bad. Real bad. But the chances of what might happen if I didn't do this forced me to push open the door.

There just was too much at stake—Izzy's life, for example.

The door slowly opened, and the scent of fairy dust and vanilla filled my senses. It was Izzy's scent. At once I felt a sense of dread as well as guilt. I shouldn't be here. But I was. So I took two quick steps into the brownstone.

Izzy had definitely come a long way in the last year. When I first met her she was living in a one-room apartment above a fairy-dust shooting gallery. A place so gritty and dangerous the bedbugs infesting the rest of the city refused to visit. But now she lived in an uptown three-floor brownstone built sometime a century ago, around the same time her great-grandmother had freed the fairies from the Shadows.

I had to admit the brownstone was very nice, as were her furnishings and other assorted knickknacks. The first floor was decorated in a pale peach color. It housed the kitchen, a dining room big enough to fit my entire apartment in, and a living area that looked untouched. In fact, most of the first floor appeared unlived-in. Not surprising since Izzy wasn't much of a cook. The last time she cooked me dinner I'd ended up in the emergency room. And it wasn't for food poisoning. Izzy had accidently stabbed me in the hand while chopping a red pepper.

At the time I was standing in an entirely different room from her.

A stack of files sat on the coffee table in the living room. I quickly flipped through them for the slightest clue as to the identity of her secret case. I paused on one file in particular. A familiar-looking file. A file I'd believed had burned up in the fire at my office.

Electrical current rushed through me when the full ramification hit me. What the hell was Izzy doing with my file? The electricity amped up to white-hot. Luckily for me, I was wearing gloves, or else the file would've burst into flames. For real this time.

Before I set the whole place ablaze, the dead bolt on the front door began to turn. Izzy was home. I froze, the file—my fucking file—in my hand. My head swiveled around the room, then to the door, searching for an escape. Izzy finding me here would be bad. Very bad.

I glared down at the file.

Before the dead bolt turned all the way, I ducked into the coat closet off the hallway next to the living room. Voices sounded in the hallway, and then Izzy let out a laugh. A real laugh. One I hadn't heard in a while, relaxed and filled with genuine humor. Izzy's date started to speak. I instantly recognized his voice, and my worst fears were confirmed. Izzy was dating our VP. Boyer & Davis was more than a figment of Grumpy's scotch-soaked mind.

My fist clenched.

Clark was saying, his voice as smooth as silk, "I'd love a glass of wine. Thank you."

"I'll be right back," Izzy answered. "Make yourself comfortable."

Not too comfortable, I thought, as beads of sweat dotted my forehead.

I could hear Clark move around, probably slipping off his expensive jacket and unbuttoning his shirt in anticipation. The soft rustling set my teeth on edge. Just how much was he anticipating? I pictured Izzy in his arms and the electricity already buzzing through me increased by tenfold. I bit my lip as my body burned with anger and— what I would never admit to anyone else—a wee bit of jealousy.

The rustling stopped when Izzy returned.

"I hope you like it," she said in a husky whisper.

Clark gave a soft chuckle. "Oh, yes."

Izzy joined in with a sultry laugh. And my insides burned as I gripped the file in my hand tighter, so much so that I nearly missed Izzy's next words. "Do you smell that?" she asked.

I winced. Damn her fairy senses.

"Smell what?" Clark asked.

"Cigarette smoke," she said quietly.

I sniffed my jacket, frowning. Shit, it did reek of cigarette smoke. I glanced down, noticing that my pocket, where I'd stuffed the cigarette butt, had started to smolder. I slapped at the pocket until the smoking stopped.

"I don't smell anything." Clark was saying. "Did you accidently leave the stove on or an iron?"

"No," she said. I pictured Izzy's forehead wrinkling as she sniffed the air, unable to pinpoint the source. "Never mind," she said, her tone relaxing. "Tell me more about your family. It must've been great growing up a Boyer." Just because the Boyer family owned more than half the real estate in New Never City didn't make for a wonderful life. Hell, I bet Clark had never burned down an entire orphanage at the age of eight.

Like an addict at a Fairy Dust Anonymous meeting, Clark launched into one story after another about his childhood. I yawned, bored by his rich-boy-next-door tales. The guy sounded way too good to be true. If I took him at his word, he'd led a charmed life filled with loving parents, a doting grandfather and uncle, and a houseful of valued and respected servants. According to him, his only problem was that he'd never met Ms. Right. A line if I'd ever heard one. Poor little rich boy. "And we never did find the cat," he finished yet another story.

Izzy laughed and my body stiffened.

"Can I ask you a question?' Clark asked hesitantly.

"They're real," she said. "My wings, I mean."

He let out a chuckle. "I knew that the moment I first saw them. But that wasn't what I wanted to know." The sofa squeaked as they moved closer to each other. I gripped the file tighter. "Izzy," Clark said. "What's with you and Reynolds? Are you two . . ."

Izzy started to laugh. "Of course not. We're partners. That's all."

Even though I'd said the same thing over and over again, hearing Izzy say it sent a rush of electrical current much like an icy shower along my nerve endings. I took a deep breath, easing the rising tension before I exploded.

"Are you sure?" Clark asked. "I don't want to get in between the two of you if . . ."

"Blue and I . . ." She paused. "We've been through a lot over the last year. And now with James . . . I'm worried about him . . ."

"I'm sure Reynolds can take care of himself," Clark said. I appreciated his faith in my abilities even through my strong desire to choke the life out of him. "How did you, of all people, get involved with a guy like him?"

What was that supposed to mean? I ripped off my gloves, rubbing my fingers together in anticipation of frying our new VP. So I wasn't some Ivy League asshole. That didn't make me pond scum. Izzy seemed to take offense to Clark's words, for she said, "Blue might look like a street thug, but he's far from it. He's smart. Smarter than he looks." She paused, finishing weakly with, "And acts."

What was that supposed to mean? My fingers clenched, wrinkling the file in my hand. Apparently she wasn't finished with her assessment of me. "He's also stubborn beyond belief. Not to mention sexist, crass, and when he sinks his teeth into a case nothing can deter him from solving it. Nothing." Her words sounded like a threat, but for the life of me I couldn't figure out why. "Which is how we met. I don't regret joining forces with Blue." She stopped and silence filled the air. "At least I didn't until recently . . ."

What? Izzy regretted our partnership? I nearly let out a bitter laugh. I wasn't the one lying and sneaking around, not to mention hiding a very important file in my brownstone. I wanted to burst from the closet and scream, Aha! like those TV detectives. But I wasn't born blue-haired yesterday. It was in my best interest to stay quiet, for now.

"What happened?" Clark asked, oozing complete sincerity.

I suspected he was weighing how much talk was left before he got some action. It had better be a lot more or else . . .

"Maybe we should talk about something else," Izzy said. "I don't want you to get the wrong impression. Reynolds & Davis Securities is a strong company and a great place to work."

Clark chuckled. "It definitely has its perks . . ."

The couch squeaked as Clark made his move. The sound of kissing filled my ears, loud and disgusting. I bet Clark slobbered. It sure as hell sounded like it. It also seemed to go on forever. Sucking noises mixed with heavy breathing. My skin began to burn. I took a deep, controlled breath, willing the current down. When that didn't work I twisted the file into a small tube. Tiny fingerprint scorch marks formed under my touch. The file began to burn. I quickly swatted the burning paper until it stopped smoking.

But it was too late to stop the fallout.

The closet door flew open.

Izzy stood in the doorway, her mouth a thin, angry line.

I glanced up from the charred file. "So how was your date?"

CHAPTER 33

"Who the hell do you think you are?" Izzy yelled her rhetorical question loud enough to wake her neighbors. A dog barked half a block away. "Get out of my closet right now!"

I did, slowly staggering to my feet, my eyes never leaving her face. She glanced at the file in my hand and then back at me. I shot her a half smile, holding out the folder like an accusing finger. "Want to tell me how you ended up with this?"

Her eyes narrowed. "What?"

I shoved the file at her. "My file, the one that supposedly burned to ash at my office. It was sitting on your coffee table."

She glanced over at the stack of files on the table. "I don't understand."

Yeah, right, and I was a going to be on the cover of *Sexiest PI* magazine. "You're lying, Izzy. What were you doing with my file that supposedly burned up in a very convenient fire?" Since some kind of file had ended up a pile of ash in my desk, I had a sneaking suspicion said fire was set by my colleague in order to cover up her theft. But why? What did she want with it? And why go as far as to set a fire to hide it?

Her face scrunched with righteous anger. "I am not a liar. I didn't even know it was there." She paused, her eyes growing wide. "James," she said, snapping her fingers. "He must've accidently put it in with my files before he . . ."

My eyes narrowed. I wanted to believe her. It would make things so much easier, but doubt burned in my brain like an electrical tide. But now wasn't the time to argue about it, mostly because Clark had squared off in front of me. I grinned in response. If he wanted a fight,

I'd damn well give him one. In fact I was aching for just this moment. My fingers curled into tight fists.

"What are you, some kind of pervert?" he growled, raising his own fists. "Hiding in the back of a closet waiting to attack? Or were you getting your rocks off listening to Isabella and me?"

Given that I was, in fact, formerly hiding in said closet, the guy had a point. But I was angry enough about finding my file in Izzy's brownstone, not to mention suffering through a disturbing amount of slobbering noises, to care. Since I couldn't very well beat the wings off my partner for her betrayal as well as poor taste in men, I'd do the next best thing—beat the stuffing out of our VP. That had a very nice ring to it.

Much to my dismay, Izzy stepped between the two of us before any bloodshed could commence. "Out. Now," she ordered me.

I lowered my fists. "But—"

"Now, Blue," she repeated, pointing toward the door.

Over her shoulder Clark flashed a satisfied smirk at my being tossed out on my ass, a smirk that didn't last long when she ordered him outside too. "If you're going to act like children, you both can leave," she said, slamming the door after us.

Outside, as the cold night air settled between us, Clark glanced at me. "Women."

I laughed, shaking my head slightly. "Fairies."

For the life of me I couldn't understand how I ended up sitting in a darkened bar, drinking whiskey with Clark Boyer the fucking Third. But here I was, matching Clark shot for shot. The bar itself was unremarkable, small and cramped, with décor from sometime in the last century. Though it offered the very best in watered-down whiskey and stale peanuts. After chipping my back tooth I pushed the peanuts away, focusing on the dark-haired man on the stool next to me.

"So, you and Izzy, huh?" I asked, slurring my words only slightly.

Clark took a drink from a snifter of watered-down brandy. "She sure is something. When we're together all I want—"

"Another round," I ordered, cutting him off.

He snorted. "What about you? The two of you ever . . . ?"

I thought of the kiss Izzy and I shared last year and shook my head. It had meant nothing, I told myself for the hundredth time, a reaction to adrenaline and near death. Nothing more. "Nope. Never."

"That's exactly what Isabella said." He paused, watching me through unfocused eyes. "Word for word in fact."

For the sake of our working relationship as well as Izzy's future with Clark, I changed the subject. Whatever Izzy and I had wasn't something I couldn't explain, and it sure as hell wasn't something I planned to share with the guy Izzy was dating. "Tell me something," I said.

Clark glanced up, eyes red rimmed. "Anything."

I blinked a few times, trying to remember what I wanted to ask. "How did a guy like you, a Boyer of the New Never City Boyers, end up working for a PI?"

"With," he snapped. "Working with."

I rolled my eyes. "Fine. Working with a PI."

He shrugged. "Karma, I guess."

I snorted. "Right."

He laughed too. "Do you have any idea what it's like growing up a Boyer?"

My mind flashed to the orphanage, before the fire, the only place a nameless kid had ever called home, as I tried to summon even the smallest amount of sympathy for him. "Yeah, I bet it was real tough. All that money and servants at your beck and call."

Pushing up from the barstool, he straightened to his full height, swaying a little. "From my earliest memory I was never good enough. I wasn't a real Boyer. I wasn't the prodigal grandson and I never could measure up to my esteemed cousin. No matter how much I tried." He paused, his eyes steady on mine. Unfortunately it was the only steady part of him. He stumbled once, twice, and then hit the floor, still mumbling about karma and the perils of being a rich white guy.

I grinned, finishing off my whiskey in a single gulp. Intense relief filled me. Clark wouldn't be marrying Izzy like the twins believed. Nor was Izzy going to dump me as a partner in favor of dear old Clark as Grump had warned. I knew this for sure. Izzy needed a man who could hold his liquor better, for living with her was bound to drive her lover to drink.

I leapt from my barstool, pulled on a pair of thick leather gloves, and helped Clark to his unsteady feet. "It's time we got you home," I said, shifting my gait to accommodate his wobbly balance.

Clark wasn't such a bad guy after all, I thought.

And then he puked all over my boots.

CHAPTER 34

I hailed a taxi outside the bar. Or more to the point, I attempted to hail a taxi. But it was after midnight, and I was a blue-haired thug carrying a guy wearing loafers. Therefore I had better odds of being struck by lightning than getting a cab. I glanced up at the night sky, thankful there wasn't a cloud in sight.

Hefting Clark's deadweight to my other arm, I half walked/half dragged him two blocks to the Fey Train station. He mumbled incoherently, which brought a smile to my lips. The evening hadn't gone as the poor bastard had hoped. Rather than holding Izzy in his arms, he had the puke-splattered likes of me holding him up. Maybe it was harder to be a Boyer than I'd thought.

Since I couldn't just leave him on the Fey Train in this condition, I pulled out my cell phone to look up his home address. Not surprisingly Clark resided uptown in a fancy loft apartment in a building built by his family more than a hundred years ago. A place with armed doormen and a concierge service at the tenants' beck and call. Even though the trip uptown would take me an hour out of the way from home, I dragged Clark aboard the train and off we went.

Half an hour later I staggered under Clark's weight as we headed up the well-lit and very clean street. Gone were the scents of urine and body odor, replaced with the fresh scents of pine and money. Luckily for me, most of the people we passed on the paved-in-gold street knew the man in my arms. Otherwise I suspect I would've been shot on sight.

When we finally arrived at Clark's expensive abode, I took a deep breath before I dug my hand into his pocket for his keys. Thankfully, by this time, Clark was completely unconscious. His head lolled to one side, and a bit of drool slipped from his lips. If Izzy saw him now she would never date his sorry ass again. I grabbed my phone, snapping a selfie of Clark and me just in case.

Once I got the door to his loft open, I pulled him inside and dropped him on the floor just inside his door. Let his maid drag him to bed. I planned to turn around and leave, but two things made me change my mind—the aroma of roasted meat and my bladder, but not in that order.

"Mind if I use your head?" I asked Clark, who let out a loud snore in response. Taking that as a yes, I left him in search of a bathroom I suspected was bigger than my entire office. When I found it I wasn't disappointed. The room was at least twice the size of my and Izzy's offices combined. A toilet sat toward the very back. I half ran to it, flipping open the lid in preparation, when a woman's voice called out, "Hello."

I quickly shoved my dick back in my pants and looked around for the chick. I soon realized the voice had come from the toilet when the sound of a babbling brook filled the room. With a sigh, I finished what I came for and then moved to the sink to wash my hands. I half expected the sink to talk to me as well and was sort of disappointed when it stayed silent.

I finished washing my hands and then glanced in the mirror. "No," I said to myself as temptation filled me. But I couldn't stop the investigator inside. I pulled on the mirror, revealing the medicine cabinet behind it. Though I was hoping for an array of embarrassing tubes and creams, I found only a handful of prescription medications, a whole lot of hair gel, and an unopened box of hair dye. Midnight black. None of which came as a surprise. I'd suspected Clark had a mean streak of vanity the first time I'd met him. His clothes and perfectly kept hair had told me—a trained investigator—as much.

Though I was ashamed to admit it, in high school I'd dabbled a bit, experimenting with whatever new product I could get my hands on. But none of them ever covered the natural color of my hair for longer than a few days. I'd tried every color known to man, from the blackest of blacks to ginger red. Then, much to my dismay, a few days after I'd dyed my hair, the blue would start to show through. I'd finally given up after a dye job left me with a splotchy red rash up and down my face, along with purple eyebrows.

I'd only wanted to fit in.

To be laughed at and teased for being an awkward teen with zits rather than an electrical menace. I had a feeling Clark knew nothing about being an awkward teen or living with faulty wiring like myself. I suspected he dyed his hair for very different reasons, namely, to get into a certain fairy's panties.

What did Izzy see in him? I wondered for the tenth time today. Though I had to admit he wasn't nearly the rich, empty-headed pretty boy I'd first thought, even if he couldn't hold his liquor.

Was it the money? I shook my head. It wasn't like Izzy was hurting for cash. Reynolds & Davis was a complete success. In another year she could buy a loft right next door if she wanted. Though I had a feeling the co-op board might have something to say about a fairy living in their midst. Was that it, then? Was Izzy dating Clark as some sort of way to gain legitimacy? Ridiculous. Izzy had been the freaking Tooth Fairy for goodness' sake.

Who cared what anyone else thought? I figured I'd tell her that tomorrow morning. And then she could forget all about Clark Boyer.

Except when it came time for our monthly marketing meeting.

I shut the medicine cabinet and left the bathroom.

I swore the toilet waved good-bye.

It was good to be Clark.

Unless one considered the hangover he would have come morning. The sides of my mouth curved into a smile at the thought.

CHAPTER 35

And not so good to be Blue, either. I groaned two hours later when a knock sounded at my apartment door. A very loud knock. I closed my eyes, hoping whoever it was at the door would have mercy on me and go away. After all, I'd just dropped into bed less than half an hour ago and had yet to reach full REM sleep. No rest for the blue haired and wicked, though, as the pounding continued, and for a moment, I wasn't sure if it was internal or external. My head felt much like Humpty Dumpty after his fall from grace. A much-deserved fall too. After all, what sort of idiot took a selfie while smoking fairy dust in a hotel room with three hookers?

Even I knew better.

I staggered from my bed after another round of knocking accompanied by a bout of loud swearing aimed at my naughty bits. Rubbing my hands together, I prepared for whatever evil intentions my visitor had in store. With a deep breath to clear my whiskey-soaked brain, I threw the door wide and then froze at the sight in front of me. "What the hell?" I yelled, ushering a half-naked Izzy, a towel wrapped around her body and her wings drenched with water, inside my apartment. "Are you all right?"

Clumps of wet hair hung around her, nearly obscuring her beautiful and soot-stained face. She waved a hand at the door and the blackened towel wrapped around her slipped a few inches, showing off way more than a nice set of wings. With supreme effort I glanced away. "Why didn't you answer the door?" she screamed. "I was standing out there while your degenerate neighbors took photos for ten minutes."

"Sorry," I said. "I didn't hear you." Over the marching band in my brain, I added silently. The less she knew about my bonding experience with Clark, the better. Hell, the less anyone knew about it . . .

"What happened?" I asked.

She clutched the towel tighter. "Can I borrow some clothes?"

"Yeah. Of course," I said, motioning to my bedroom. Izzy ran past me, disappearing behind my makeshift door, which was nothing more than a rubber ducky shower curtain and duct tape. The sound of drawers opening and closing echoed from the room. I imaged Izzy standing naked in my bedroom, and electrical heat pulsed through me. I swallowed hard, disgusted with myself. Izzy was obviously distressed. It was not the time to picture her naked, in my bedroom, where my bed sat only a few feet away . . .

Hell, I must still be drunk.

"Blue," she said as she came out dressed in a pair of my boxer shorts and a T-shirt that hit her midthigh, "everything's gone. Destroyed. What am I going to do?"

I shook off my bedroom fantasy and focused on what she was saying. "What happened?" I asked again.

She gazed up at me, her eyes dewy with tears. "My brownstone burned down. To the cellar, Blue. Nothing was left." She paused, choking up. "I barely made it out alive."

CHAPTER 36

I stood at the side of my bed watching Izzy sleep. She moaned and her wings fluttered, sending up a cloud of toxic fairy dust, but she didn't wake. I shook my head, swallowing back a hundred terrifying thoughts about what could've happened to her. Two fires and one burned intern were much more than a coincidence.

Yeah, I was an investigative genius.

After she'd settled in with a very large tumbler of whiskey, she had walked me through the events leading up to the fire and then immediately following. Once Clark and I had left, she changed out of her "date" attire. I could only assume that her "date" attire included sexy lingerie, the kind women rarely wore outside catalogs and those sexy Golden Goose's Secret commercials. (FYI, after an investigation two months ago I knew that Goose had much more than that one secret.) Not that I had much experience with upscale lingerie. My dates opted for inedible, nonconductive undies and rubber gloves.

After a quick shower Izzy had heard someone or something rustling around on the first floor. She grabbed a baseball bat and started down the stairs. I began to lecture her about the dangers of confronting an intruder, in nothing but a towel, but she waved me off. "I can take care of myself," she said, her voice sounding as if she'd chewed broken glass. "How many times do I have to say it?"

I ignored her comment, asking what happened once she came down the stairs. "It was dark so I couldn't see anyone, but I smelled smoke." She paused, her eyes taking on a faraway look. "I grabbed a few things, like my purse and some cash, and ran out the door while dialing nine-one-one on my cell phone. My hands were shaking so badly I couldn't dial the nine."

"You grabbed your cell but forgot to put on some clothes?" I asked, my eyebrow arching. Izzy wasn't being completely honest. I could tell by the way she enhanced her story, adding details to cement it. It was Liar 101. "What aren't you telling me, Izzy?"

She glanced right and then left, swallowing hard before answering. "Your file . . . The one with all the information about your birth . . ."

The one I'd stupidly left at her place when she tossed me out.

"I'm sorry, Blue . . . It was destroyed in the fire . . ." She licked her dry lips. "For real this time."

As the sun hit the top of the sky I lit a cigarette, annoying the patrons surrounding me in the outdoor café. Good. The farther away people stayed, the better. I fingered the gun in my pocket. Someone had nearly killed Izzy last night. The attempt on my own life, which resulted in James's death, was one thing. But harming even a hair on Izzy's fiery red head was the last mistake whoever was behind this mess would make. I would destroy them. Not just kill, but twist them into a pretzel and then rip out their . . . some body part or other.

Let's call it assassin's choice.

Izzy joined me at the table waving a hand in front of her face. "Blue," she yelled. "You said you'd quit."

I shook my head, taking another drag. "That's what you're concerned about right now?"

"Oh, forgive me for being worried about your health," she said flopping down in the seat across from me. She took a long drink of her iced coffee before addressing me again. "It was my brownstone that burned to the ground. So what has your boxers in a bunch?"

I laughed. "My boxers are not in a bunch, as you put it. But yes, I'm a little on edge. After all," I said, my voice rising with each word, "someone almost killed you." The very thought chilled me as no other. Keeping Izzy safe was top priority. Forget the missing fairies. Nothing mattered to me more than protecting Izzy from a killer. But to accomplish that goal, I first had to find out who had killed James and why.

"Keep your voice down," she said. "Yes, it looks like we're in someone's sights. But instead of going all vigilante, let's find out why and then we can decide what to do about it." She stopped, her eyes on mine. "Together, Blue."

I agreed with a small shake of my head, mostly to shut her up. No way would I risk her life. This was my case and mine alone. I planned to do some very permanent damage to the villain responsible. Not that I'd share my plans with her. It would only upset her.

I smiled in anticipation.

Izzy returned my smile with a satisfied grin of her own.

A shiver of warning sent the hairs on the back of my neck rising.

CHAPTER 37

A few hours later, Izzy safely tucked away at Reynolds & Davis, I hit the streets for some old-fashioned investigating. Sadly I wasn't alone. Izzy had insisted, by blackmailing me, that I bring our genius albeit clumsy investigator, Alice, along for the ride once she learned of my destination. "Are you crazy?" Izzy had yelled loud enough to wake the lawyers one floor below.

"No." I folded my arms over my chest. "I don't like it any more than you do, but I have to do this. It's the only way."

"Damn you, Blue," she cursed. "If you get yourself killed . . ."

"I won't."

"Fine," she said. "If you insist on this asinine mission, then I'm coming with you."

The merely thought of involving Izzy in more danger had my hair turning that weird bluish grey color favored by women of a certain age. "No way." I ended our conversation by turning and walking out of her office. She stormed after me. "Blue . . ."

I kept walking.

Finally Izzy relented. "Okay. You win. I won't join you. But you have to take Alice with you. She'll watch your back."

I slowly turned around to face her. "You trust her?"

"With your life," Izzy responded.

And with that, I found myself standing on the street with Alice at my side rather than my fairyguards, who were now glued to Izzy's side despite her very loud, screeching protests. I wasn't about to take another chance on Izzy's safety.

"You follow my lead," I said to Alice for the tenth time since we'd left Reynolds & Davis. She glanced up, her glasses slipping down her nose. She pushed them back in place before answering, "This isn't my first investigation, Mr. Reynolds."

"Blue," I said. "If we're going to be working together, you need to call me Blue. And above all else, watch your back. This is serious. One man is already dead. Who knows what we're going to find inside." I gave an affected shiver to emphasis the horrors that might wait.

"I know," she said. "Don't worry. I'm well aware of the danger."

"Good." I shot her a small smile. "Then, let's do this."

She nodded once, and together we headed for our target.

Little Bo Peep's apartment in the sky.

If anyone knew anything about what had happened over the last week, it would be Peep. The night Izzy caught Peep and me together, Peep had gotten me there by claiming she had information about James's murder. Now I planned on finding out exactly what she'd meant, even if I killed a few sheep in the process. If only I could get past the doorman.

Peep was meticulous about her security, probably because even those who called her a friend wanted to see her six feet under. I stepped inside the building and quickly found myself surrounded by eight guns pointed at various nonblue parts of my body.

I held up my gloved hands. "Take it easy, boys," I said. "I come in peace."

"Ha," snorted one of the guards with a blank spot where his left eyebrow should be.

"I'm here to talk to Bo Peep." I shot them all my most innocent of smiles as I pulled off my gloves. "Just talk. No one needs to get hurt."

All the guards took a collective step back.

The guard with the off-putting lack of eyebrow shook his gun at me. "That's what you told me three months ago."

I snapped my fingers. "Now I remember. Sorry, I couldn't place you without the other brow." Unfortunately for him, a few months ago the guard and I had a brief altercation involving my frying off various bits of his facial hair after he'd accused me of stealing from an upscale men's store. I'd naturally taken offense at his blue-haired profiling. It only escalated from there, until I sent fifty thousand volts through his badge-heavy body.

Before things turned ugly—or uglier, as one eyebrow didn't look good on anyone—I noticed a slight woman edging her way toward the nearest guard. I made shooing motions with my head. But Alice didn't listen. Instead she moved even closer and then promptly disappeared. I frowned, not so much at her disappearing act but at the police baton jamming into my sternum. It was quickly followed up with a smack to my left knee. I dropped to the ground, stifling a scream. Good thing too, since Bo Peep's voice crackled, barely discernable, from the speaker on the security console. "Please show Mr. Reynolds and his Girl Friday to my penthouse."

Girl Friday? I rolled my eyes. Alice really needed to work on her PI slang.

Not that the guards thought so. They quickly jumped to attention, lowering their weapons and ushering me as well as my supposed Girl Friday, Alice, who suddenly appeared at my side, into the elevator. I held my smile in place until the doors closed.

"Damn it, Alice," I began, spinning toward her. "I had everything under control. I didn't need you to interfere."

"Yes, I could see that, sir," she said without a hint of sarcasm. "Why, you had them just where you wanted them."

Little did she know, but I had. Sometimes in my business you took a beating as a way of making amends. I'd cost the one-eyebrow guard more than just his brow. I'd cost him his job too. Not to mention his pride. Letting him smack me with a baton a few times made up for that. I could've explained all of this to Alice, but being a chick, she would never comprehend the vast inner workings of the male mind.

But she had gotten us inside with her Bo Peep impersonation.

I shook my head at her as we rode the elevator toward Bo Peep's penthouse. "I'll let it go this time, but next time I tell you to wait outside until I give the all clear, you do it."

She nodded. "Yes, sir."

"Blue," I reminded her.

"Yes, Blue," she corrected herself.

After a moment of awkward silence, I licked my lips and then, against my better judgment, asked her just how she'd managed to hack the intercom to make it sound like Bo Peep had invited us upstairs. I sighed as my judgment proved right and Alice launched into a long-winded explanation of circuits, physics, and a bunch of other terms used to put those of us with IQs under 160 in our place.

Halfway through her tale I longed for a sharp stick in the eye.

But rather than a sharpened stick, a much bigger pain materialized in the sexy form of Bo Peep as the elevator door slid wide. "Well, hello, Blue." Her smile widened as she looked me up and down like I was the flavor of the week. "Look who came back for more."

I shook my head, stepping out of the elevator and into Bo's opulent penthouse. The room itself looked much like it had a few days ago. Floor-to-ceiling windows gleamed against the backdrop of the city. Expensive artwork lined every wall, showing off both the taste and wealth of the woman standing in front of me, a woman who was staring at Alice, her eyebrow arched as if considering some nefarious plan. I stepped between the two women, gaining Peep's attention before she talked Alice into working at her Peep show.

Bo reached her hand out, running her finger down my tie. "I see you've traded up."

My eyes narrowed. "Excuse me?"

"This one"—she pointed to Alice—"for the other one. The bitchy one with wings. Smart move."

"This one"—Alice stepped from behind me, her eyes blazing behind her glasses—"has a name. And"—her eyes flickered over my face—"better taste in men."

I winced. "You do know I'm standing right here . . ."

Alice stepped closer to Bo as if to intimidate the older woman. But Bo wasn't a pushover. She stood her ground, leaving Alice and her nose to nose. Neither woman backed down, and tension filled the air. Something more was going on here just below the surface. Something I was missing, which, given the number of X and Y chromosomes in the room, I was fairly used to. I cleared my throat to gain their attention. "Ladies," I said, "why don't we take a seat? Bo"—I motioned to the couch, half expecting her to shank Alice with the nearest sheep-sharpened object instead—"I wanted to ask you a few questions."

"That's all you want anymore, Blue," Bo said, blowing out a long-suffering sigh, but she did as I asked, taking a seat on her plush leather sofa.

Once she was seated, I motioned for Alice to wait by the elevator, for two reasons. The first was to keep her as far away from Bo as possible, and the second, to make sure no sudden surprises appeared like the last time I was here. Though I knew for a fact Izzy was back at the office and that Right and Left would keep her there. But who knew what Bo had up her wool sleeves.

Bo shifted on the couch, crossing her long, tanned legs. For a moment, my mind went blank, and judging by the gleam in her eyes, I might've let out a little drool. I shook off the rising electrical heat inside me. Bo wouldn't get to me. Not this time. "No games, Peep. I need answers. Now."

She leaned in. "I have answers to all sorts of things. What, exactly, did you want to know?"

I swallowed, shaking my head. "Do you know who killed James or not?"

"Maybe," she said, sliding her hand up my thigh. "Maybe not."

I pushed her away. "Stop playing around. This is serious."

"If you say so."

God, I was stupid. Peep knew nothing about James's murder. She had led me to her penthouse with promises of finding James's killer, but she'd really had another motive in mind. "Why did you invite me up here the other night? Was it so Izzy would find us? Did you think it would matter to her?"

Bo laughed, a wicked-sounding cackle. "You think your relationship or lack thereof with Isabella Davis means anything to me? You know me better than that."

I did indeed. Bo never did anything for free. A piece of the puzzle clicked into place. "Someone paid you to set me up."

Her smile grew.

"Why?" I asked, more to myself than to the greedy, sheep-hoarding witch next to me. I hadn't expected her to answer, so I was surprised when she leaned back against the soft leather and began to speak.

"I got a call a few hours before I contacted you," she said.

"From who?"

She shrugged. "I didn't recognize the voice. But it was a man . . . I think . . ."

"You're not sure?"

Her lips flattened to an unflattering thin line. "The caller was disguising his voice. It sounded almost mechanical, like a computer."

I considered how easy it was for Alice to use the intercom to affect Bo Peep's voice. Was it that easy for the caller? I frowned. "What did the caller want?" I asked, though I had a pretty good idea. The caller wanted Izzy to find me with Bo. And that meant the caller knew my sheepish history with Bo Peep. I wasn't sure what the caller had expected to happen. Maybe he—or possibly the mysterious blonde whom the Ferns saw, if she had disguised her voice—wanted to ruin my and Izzy's partnership? As if a simple roll in the wool would have any impact.

"He wanted your girlfriend to find you in a compromising situation," Peep said. "I told him it would cost him, and I named a price. Ten minutes later, my bank account had a nice chunk of change deposited, and I had a call to make."

I shook my head, disgusted. "How much?"

"Ten grand."

My eyes narrowed. That was a little more than a chunk of change. "That's a lot of dough for a simple setup."

She shrugged again. "Express charge."

"What?"

"He wanted it done right then." She frowned, shivering a little in the sunlit room. "Insisted on it, as a matter of fact."

CHAPTER 38

"What do you think?" I asked Alice as we rode the elevator down to the lobby.

She glanced up from the small smartphone screen in her hand, the glare of electronic light flickering off her glasses. "Are you stupid? That woman is evil. Why would you pick her over Ms. Davis?"

I bit my lip to avoid shouting. Through clenched teeth, I growled, "I didn't pick Bo over Izzy. I'm not involved with Peep." Not anymore at least. "And Izzy and I are partners. That's all."

"Yeah, right," Alice snorted. "Everyone at the office knows about you two. It's the talk of the water cooler. Well, it was until I tripped and broke the damn thing. You should really think about installing skid-proof rugs."

Or hire more coordinated employees.

"Shit," I said under my breath as a sudden thought occurred to me. Whoever had set me up must work at Reynolds & Davis. No one else would be privy to the tempestuous relationship Izzy and I had shared over the last few months, let alone the fact that Izzy had my file at her place. I said as much to Alice, who looked at me and laughed. Loudly, I might add. When she quieted, I asked, "What's so funny?"

She used the back of her hand to wipe away an affected tear. "You." When my eyes narrowed, her amusement died, as did her insubordination. She shot me a sheepish smile. "Sorry. I thought we were bonding." Since I didn't bother with a response, she quickly added, "Guess not. Anyway, I merely wanted to point out that those of us"—she paused—"lucky enough to be employed at Reynolds & Davis, since it's a great company to work—"

"Enough with the kissing up." I stepped closer to her. "Just tell me why you think it's not someone at the company."

"Yes, sir." She snapped to attention. "We're not the only ones aware of your and Ms. Davis's relationship." She quickly went on before I could argue. "Or lack of relationship outside your very professional and not at all messy partnership."

"Damn it," I muttered.

"Sir?"

I shook my head slowly, as if reaching a long-overdue conclusion. "I told Izzy we shouldn't hire you, but did she listen? No. Like everything else, I let her have her way, and now this . . ." Alice's face paled, and I grinned. "I'm kidding," I said when she looked ready to faint. "But you're right." Our employees weren't the only suspects. Any number of fairies, as well as the dwarfs on the Fairy Council, had knowledge as well as a whole lot of motive to destroy Izzy's and my partnership.

Electrical current spiraled inside me. I was no closer to solving the question of who was behind the fires and James's murder than I was when Alice and I left the office an hour ago. Alice must've felt the rise in tension as well as the temperature of the elevator, for she cleared her throat to gain my attention. "We could always check the phone records. Maybe see where the call to Peep originated from?"

"Huh," I said. "Guess you just might earn your paycheck after all."

CHAPTER 39

Dusk had started to turn the pollution-riddled sky from bright orange to golden when Izzy knocked on my office door an hour later. She shot me a faint smile, nodding at the scorched fingerprints on the top of the brand-new desk she'd purchased that morning. "Making yourself at home, I see."

I winced, swiping my sleeve over the burn marks. "Sorry about those. I was thinking about something Alice said earlier."

"About the case?"

I licked my lips. "No."

Izzy's eyes narrowed as she took a seat across from me. Silk rubbing against silk whispered when she crossed her legs. "About what, then?"

"Us." I kicked my feet off the desk and straightened in my chair. Our eyes locked, and the room heated as electrical current sparked through me.

Izzy frowned, her gaze darting to the city beyond the glass windows of my office. "How did your talk with Bo Peep go? Did she know who's behind this?"

Annoyance flashed through me. I didn't want to talk about the case, about the fires, about death and destruction. Not now. But the tilt of Izzy's jaw told me we'd be discussing it come hell or three men in bathwater. "Someone hired her to set me up." I pushed from the desk. "They wanted it done that day. As soon as possible."

Her frown deepened. "I don't understand. Someone hired Bo to sleep with you?"

"No," I said sharply. "Someone wanted you to find Bo and me together."

"That makes even less sense." She stroked her chin between her thumb and forefinger. "I can see someone thinking you need a little help getting laid . . ."

"Funny," I said. "But this is serious, Izzy. Someone thought"—I paused, weighing my next words—"for some reason, that you might be jealous—"

"No." Izzy leapt from her seat, pacing back and forth. Before I could question her, Alice pushed open my office door. She still wore the same outfit she had earlier, but her hair now hung loosely around her face. A pen was tucked behind her ear. "I got it," she said in a near squeal.

I rolled my eyes, annoyed by both her tone and the interruption.

Alice didn't seem to notice; instead she flounced inside the office waving her arms. "The call came from within half a block."

Whoopee. So the guy who called Peep was close to her. Big deal. "Alice," I said in warning. "Do you have anything else? Something useful maybe? Like the name of the caller?" I knew I was taking my bad mood out on her, a girl who'd been nothing but helpful. A part of me felt bad too. But the rest damn well wanted more from her than a location that did us no good. Electricity crackled in the air.

Alice's smile slipped an inch, eyes widening. "I'm sorry."

I blew out a harsh breath. "No, I'm sorry. This isn't your fault. None of it. Why don't you take off. Go home. Get some sleep and we'll investigate more in the morning." Late morning, I thought, as I had plans to take a little trip to Fairyland. Since I hadn't made any headway in finding the person responsible for setting fire to my office as well as Izzy's brownstone, I decided to focus my *energy* on another, shorter case. The Fairy Council seemed like a good place to start kicking dwarf ass to get some answers about the possible fairy-nappings. Hell, even if I didn't get any answers I'd feel much better after. I cracked my knuckles in anticipation.

"But, sir," Alice said, "you don't understand."

I raised an eyebrow, both at her use of "sir" and at her comment. "What? What is it I don't get?"

She glanced from me to Izzy, who was now pacing my office, her wings fluttering faster and faster. Izzy appeared lost in her own thoughts, oblivious to anything Alice or I said. Which was fine with me. Alice took two steps closer to me, her voice lowering to a near whisper, "The caller wasn't half a block from Peep's penthouse, sir. But here. Within a half-block radius."

Her words smacked into me like lightning, causing electricity to flame from my fingers. I quickly jumped up, stepping on the errant strikes now sizzling my newly renovated office. All this time I'd figured someone wanted Izzy to catch me with Peep, but that wasn't the case at all. Whoever had called had something less sinister in mind but a hell of a lot more twisted. "Aw, hell," I said. "Izzy," I called to my partner in noncrime, "we really have to get better security."

CHAPTER 40

I filled a crystal glass to the rim with whiskey, the good stuff reserved for nights like this. Nights when everything I'd once believed now lay in shambles beneath my feet. Izzy sat in the chair across from me, my desk the only physical barrier between us. It might as well have been an ocean. "I don't believe it," she said for the fourth time since Alice had left my office after dropping the phone-call bombshell. "Setting you up with Peep seems like a lot of work for someone to go through just to get me out of the office."

I nodded. She wasn't wrong. The caller had gone to a lot of trouble. But I knew it was the truth. The caller had wanted something in our office, wanted something so badly that he or she had risked breaking and entering to get it, and when that didn't work, said caller set fire to my office in hopes of either destroying whatever it was he or she wanted or hiding the evidence of the break-in. Either way, the caller had made one mistake.

Trusting Peep to keep quiet.

I let out a small smile. Hell, I almost sympathized with the bad guy, having been a victim of Bo's less-than-high moral values.

So what was it this person wanted?

Izzy seemed to be thinking the same thing as she pushed to her feet and glared at me. "If what you think is true, what was it the intruder wanted?"

I shrugged. "Who knows?" Though I had a sneaking suspicion what it was, a suspicion that sent bolts of current along my nerves. I hoped—no, I prayed—I was wrong, that the caller had wanted something else, something far less personal.

But Izzy wasn't buying my casual shrug. "Let's not play games, Blue. It was your office they burned."

"So?" I blinked up at her with innocence.

"So," she growled, "they wanted something of yours. Something personal."

I tilted my head. "Personal? What makes you say that?" Even though I'd come to the same conclusion, hearing Izzy say it aloud made it seem much more real.

And terrifying.

"The setup," she said. "If they'd wanted a case file, they wouldn't have arranged the setup. After all, why bother? The caller knew you." Her lips curved into a frown. "Knew us. Our history. Your history with Peep."

"Perhaps."

"The file," she whispered. "Your file. The same one that burned up last night at my brownstone." Her eyes burned with anger. "They set fire to my place to destroy your file!"

I lifted my shoulders in a shrug.

"But how did they even know I had it?"

I shrugged again, but I worried I knew the answer and it wasn't one either of us would like. Whoever was behind this was someone we knew, someone close to us. Someone who wanted my past buried, along with whoever got in the way.

"What's our next move?" she asked, her voice barely above a whisper.

"Our?" I paused. "Don't you have your own super-secret case you should be working on?"

Her lips thinned. "I gave up on it."

"Is that so?" I grinned, feeling much more satisfied than I should've. After all, it wasn't like I was making headway on solving my current caseload. But it felt good to have Izzy back where she belonged, bossing everyone around and, for the most part, with the exception of nearly being barbecued alive, out of harm's way.

"Don't look so superior," she said. "We have a lot of investigating to do. So I repeat, where do *we* start?"

I looked away, my eyes scanning the glow of the city lights. "We start at the beginning. On the day I was born."

Thirty-one years ago a baby was born to Mr. and Mrs. Smith. Months later I was found on the steps of an orphanage by a nun named Sister Mary. And now someone desperately wanted to keep me from finding out what had happened between my birth and the day I was found on the steps. Apparently this someone had even gone the extra murderous mile when cleaning up loose ends, and instead of killing me, the greatest loose end of all, like the assassin planned, he or she had killed James. The question was, why? The file held few leads, and none of them were any good. I should know. I'd been chasing them for years.

"Blue," Izzy said as she stood up, reaching across my desk for my gloved hand and bringing me back to the present. Her fingers curled around the leather. "Please calm down. You're vibrating with current."

I nodded, taking a soothing breath and a fortifying gulp of expensive whiskey. "Sorry about that. I was thinking."

She snorted. "I could see that. And if I had my guess, none of those thoughts were of fluffy bunnies and purring kittens."

"Bunnies aren't as cuddly as you think," I said with a wince.

"I know you're angry," Izzy said. "And I don't blame you." She paused, her fingers gripping my hand tighter. "After all these years of searching for your parents—"

"I couldn't care less about my parents." I ripped my hand from her grip. "They didn't want me. I get that." I paused, tasting each word as it left my mouth. "I would've made the same decision."

"That's not true. You aren't like that." She came around my desk and grabbed the lapels of my jacket. I halfheartedly waved her off, but given that her house had burned to the cellar less than twenty-four hours ago, my heart wasn't in it. "It doesn't matter now," I said. "What matters is figuring out who knew about the file in the first place."

A half smile hovered on her lips. "You're right."

I frowned, feeling manipulated yet again, but for the life of me I couldn't say why. I shook off the feeling, focusing on the matter at hand. As far as I knew, only three people knew about the file. Two of them sat in my office, and the other was dead. Since I sure as hell didn't tell anyone about the file and Izzy wouldn't share that kind of information, that left my barbecued intern, James. Sure, he had the convenient alibi of being dead, but what if he'd told someone else about the file? And that person or persons killed him to cover up the real intended crime?

Close, I thought. But not quite right.

There was a puzzle piece still missing.

I tapped my finger against my chin. Something about James's murder bothered me. But for the life of me I couldn't put my finger on it. Whoever had done it had wanted it to look like an accident. The killer had been almost meticulous about it—with the one small exception of the rock salt.

Why didn't the killer scrub the scene clean after the murder?

Only one answer came to mind.

An answer that chilled me down to the blue hair on my toes.

The reason was simple.

It was too late. The killer was already dead.

CHAPTER 41

When I shared my theory with Izzy that James had planned to murder me that day but instead had accidently killed himself, she looked shocked, and then her expression grew murderous. "That little prick," she yelled. "We gave him a job and he repays us by trying to kill you?"

I smiled at her outrage. "Not defending his actions, but in all fairness, we didn't exactly pay him."

"He was getting college credit!"

Apparently college credit and on-the-job experience hadn't been enough for James. I suspected he'd taken to cold-blooded killing for cash as a way to afford the finer things. He must not have been very good at his murderous profession since he lived in the pigsty of a frat house in Fairyland. Not to mention his accidently electrocuting himself at my apartment.

I had to give it to Detective Locks after all.

James's death really was an accident.

Just one that happened in the course of his attempting to murder me.

If what I thought was true, I needed to figure out who had paid him to kill me in the first place. The obvious answer was someone connected to my early life. Someone who wanted to keep my past in the past. James must've told them about the file, and when he failed to kill me, James's benefactor had decided to take matters into his or her own hands, burning up my office and Izzy's brownstone until he or she finally destroyed the file. Now I was the only obstacle in erasing the past.

I turned to Izzy, curious about how far this rabbit hole went. "How did you know I was with Bo Peep the day you found us?"

"Someone left a message with Doreen before she locked up the office for the night," she said, her forehead wrinkled in thought. "It said something about you being in danger and gave me an address. Until I saw you and Peep, I had no idea it was hers."

A part of me cursed her stupidity while the other part appreciated her concern. I opted for the former part. "So you rushed out of the building without a second thought?"

She exhaled sharply, a sneer curling her lips. "I thought you were in trouble. Besides, after you ditched Right and Left in Fairyland I had no reason to doubt the caller."

Now my forehead puckered.

"What?" Izzy asked, her hands clenched in front of her. "What is it?"

"Who's Doreen?"

"Our receptionist, you idiot."

"Right." In my defense, like many of our other employees, Doreen had been working for us for only three months. Until we'd solved the missing-jewel-encrusted-mittens case we just hadn't needed the extra help. I frowned, thinking James had come aboard around the same time. As had Alice. If I remembered correctly, they'd both come highly recommended.

"Why?" Izzy asked.

"Why what?"

She rolled her big, almost violet-colored eyes. "Why did you ask about that day? Do you know something you're not sharing with the rest of the class?"

I ran my gloved hand over my chin. "Why send you out of the office?"

Izzy shrugged. "So I wouldn't catch them in the act?"

While her answer made complete sense, it just didn't sit right. Whoever this was had already paid James to kill me in cold blood, so why the sudden squeamishness at a little B and E?

Unless they wanted Izzy to be safely away.

CHAPTER 42

"Come on, Blue," Peyton squeaked. "Why would we send someone to kill you?"

"This time, you mean?" I tightened my grip around his throat, the stitches of my leather gloves leaving marks along his neck like a pitcher got when he gripped a baseball. Considering that he and his brother had tried pretty damn hard to murder me a little more than a year ago, I felt completely justified in choking him a little longer. Unfortunately Izzy didn't quite see things my way.

"Damn it, Blue." She swatted at my arm with one wing while doing her best to free Peyton from my grip with her hands. "Let him go."

"No," I said in what sounded like a reasonable tone to me.

Izzy's affected gasp suggested I'd missed the mark. "Don't talk to me like that," she said, smacking me again, this time with her hand. "Now, let him go before I . . . before I . . ."

"Nag me to death?"

Her gasp was even louder this time, and very real. I winced but didn't lessen my grip on Peyton. The little bastard had tried to kill me again. And burned up my office. I just knew it. He was somehow connected to the mystery surrounding my birth and I would damn well find out how. I squeezed even harder as his face grew a nice bluish hue.

"Think about it, Blue," Izzy was saying. "If Peyton was behind this, why would he set my brownstone on fire?"

I blinked a few times, glancing from Right and Left to the former Tooth Fairy.

"With me in it."

And with those words my theory crumbled into a pile, as did Peyton once I released him. He fell forward, but Right grabbed his arm before he hit the floor. I frowned, my gaze on Izzy. She was right. Sure the fairies would love to see me dead, but they would never risk hurting their beloved former Tooth Fairy. Someone else had started the fire at my office as well as the one at Izzy's brownstone. It was time to face the truth.

Only two people had reason to destroy my file.

And I shared 50 percent of my DNA with each.

While I never had parents, I was fairly sure most didn't go around trying to murder their electrified offspring. I slumped down farther into my couch, my gaze unfocused, much like the rest of me. I didn't want to believe it. But I couldn't ignore the truth any longer. The only people with reason to keep me from learning about my birth were the people actively involved in it. The fire at the maternity ward the night of my birth should've been clue enough. And yet, I'd buried my bluish head, slipping further and further into denial.

Until only one option remained.

Nature held true.

I was a monster born of monsters.

"Blue," Izzy called, her fingers lightly brushing my forehead. Her touch felt like heaven, until the snap, crackle, and pop of electricity buzzing through her reached my ears.

I pushed her away, finally focusing on her face. "Leave me alone." I took a shallow breath. "Please."

She shook her head. "I'm worried about you."

"Don't be."

"Too late," she whispered. "It's part of the package. I worry about you, and you do the same for me. That's what makes us such a good team."

I didn't want Izzy on my team. Not now. The more distance between us, the better. Especially since one or both of my parents were willing to kill to keep me from the truth. If anything ever happened to Izzy . . . A sudden, terrifying thought occurred to me. I wasn't the only loose end in need of being tied. There was another person who knew the truth.

Christine Connors Quick.

And I'd led them right to her.

CHAPTER 43

"Ms. Quick," I yelled to the wide, winged orderly. "Where is she?"

He blinked, a rush of emotions crossing his face as he held out a hand to stop me from entering the locked ward at the Shady Wings Nursing Home. The resulting shock when his hand made contact with the exposed skin on my forearm sent him back two steps, but he stayed on his feet. Barely.

Not bothering to wait for the door to be unlocked, I kicked it right below the lock, forcing the door open under the force. I ran through the splintered doorway in search of Christine. Izzy followed me, along with her fairyguards, Right and Left, who, much to her dismay, had been stuck like fairy glue to Izzy since the fire at her brownstone. She yelled for me to stop. "Blue," she screamed. "Please. Be careful."

I ignored her warning, my mind focused on one thing and one thing only. I had to save Christine Connors. Nothing else mattered.

But I was too late.

I pulled to a stop in front of Christine's now empty room. All the Post-it notes that once covered every surface were gone.

And I knew.

I was too late.

A fairy in a white lab coat appeared behind me. "I'm sorry for your loss."

I slowly turned around, my glare as hot as the summer sun. "She's dead," I said, no doubt in my voice. "When?"

"Yesterday," the winged nurse said. "We found her on the floor. She must've fallen out of bed and hit her head. There was nothing we could do . . ."

I stifled a snort, my body humming with violence. A convenient accident. The arsonist's MO. I wondered if Christine had recognized my parents as they snuffed the life out of her. I thought back to Christine's description of my mother and her shimmering golden hair. Was it possible that the mysterious woman the Ferns had claimed to see was in fact my very own mother? Had she and James sat in the darkened bar, plotting my demise? I knew some animals ate their young . . .

My body burned with electricity at the thought. Blowing out a harsh breath, I did my best to relax before Shady Wings became Scorched Wings. The last thing I needed was another fire.

"I'm glad you came," the fairy nurse was saying. "We searched and searched for Ms. Quick's next of kin—"

"He's not—" Izzy began.

"Not blaming Shady Wings for Ms. Quick's death," I said cutting off her denial. "Now, if you would provide us with her effects we'll be on our way." The nurse snapped to attention, nearly running down the hallway to do my biding. When she disappeared around the corner, Izzy spun to face me. "What was that all about?"

"Christine never married, never had children." I gave a sad smile. "She has no living heirs. The nursing home would just donate her clothes and toss the rest of her things in the trash."

"So?" Izzy asked, her forehead wrinkling.

I pictured my future, a lonely old man electrocuting my caregiver when I slapped her on the ass. Oddly the image didn't make me as sad as it should have. In fact, it was the first time in a very long time that I considered living to a ripe, lecherous old age. Maybe Izzy's constant nagging about my smoking, drinking, and fried (as in frying) food habits wasn't a bad thing. I shot her a small smile, returning to the topic at hand. "Christine might have left a clue somewhere in her mementos."

She closed her eyes and then slowly opened them. "Blue, I know how bad you feel, but you need to let this—"

"Here you are," the winged nurse said, passing me a box filled with clothes, thousands of Post-it notes, and something that smelled an awful lot like the dead. I took a shallow breath through my mouth as I thanked the nurse.

"I don't like this, Blue," Izzy whispered as we started to leave. "Not one bit."

That made two of us. Three of us if I counted the dead woman whose possessions I was stealing.

* * *

Hours later, day slowly shifted to night, but I didn't notice. I was too engrossed in the puzzle of Christine Connors Quick's life. Shuffling through her Post-it notes was like going a little crazy. Nothing felt solid. Or real. I found myself doubting things I'd believed true. I wondered if this was how Christine had spent the last part of her life. If so, maybe ending her suffering wasn't as tragic as I'd thought.

"Blue," Izzy called.

I glanced up, focusing on Izzy for the first time since we'd arrived at my apartment. I set down the tiny, charred-at-both-ends hospital wristband with the words ". . . ittle Baby Bl . . ." and rubbed my eyes. Exhaustion filled me like a wave. I was tired. Tired of searching for clues to my past. Tired of losing. Just plain fucking tired. "Izzy," I said, "if you're here to bitch at me, please, not now."

Izzy took a step back, as if wounded by my words. "Is that how you see me?"

When I said nothing, she slowly sat down on the couch. "I'm sorry, Blue. I'm just so worried about you. About what all of this means." She spread her arms wide across the mounds of Post-it notes and knickknacks. Her voice lowered to a whisper. "About how you're going to react to whatever it is you find. Please, stop this. Before it's too late. The past is just that. It doesn't matter. Not to me."

"I wish it was that easy." Not now. Not when those who bore me had other, much more murderous, ideas. I no longer cared as much about finding the truth behind my birth. My only thoughts were of finding the monsters responsible for it.

She gave me a small smile. "It is that easy. All you have to do is forget about what happened or didn't happen thirty years ago and focus on what you want for a future."

I slowly rose from my crouched position on the floor, considering her words. I did want a future, but I wasn't sure it was in the cards. Not now. But in that moment, with Izzy's eyes staring up at me, I wanted to reach out to her. To feel her skin against mine. Not in a lustful way—which, let's face it, was my go-to reaction—but to feel, for once, the comforting touch of another, without sending her into convulsive shock, of course. I wanted to be free, for once, from my curse.

My body seemed to have a mind of its own as I lifted my ungloved hand toward her. Thankfully I regained control and pulled back in time. But it was too late. Izzy's fingers clutched mine, the heat of her skin soothing the hurt away. My gaze flew to our collective hands. Skin to skin. Only natural, normal heat between us. That normal, natural heat quickly morphed into electricity, but not the kind I normally possessed. The electricity of longing and desire.

Izzy's lips opened slightly and I took full advantage. I tugged her forward, her lush, soft, winged body falling against mine. Taking my other hand, I pressed my thumb against her chin, both asking and demanding. Her mouth complied with my demand. And I tasted her mouth for the second time in a year.

The kiss was soft at first, both of us hesitant. Then the fire of desire took control, and the kiss heated, my hands seemingly groping every part of her body, and yet, our mouths never lost contact. I lost myself in the intoxicating scent of fairy dust and fairy. My knee slid up her inner thigh, opening her body for mine. The electric thrill sent my senses reeling.

And then with a loud crackle, Izzy went flying across the room.

Luckily her wings softened her landing, though she sat there dazed for a few minutes. I ran to her, pulling to a stop before touching her again. "Are you all right?" I asked, fear turning my question into a growl.

She blinked up at me. "I saw stars."

"What can I say? I have that effect on women." Probably the wrong thing to say to the woman I'd nearly killed, but Izzy wasn't any woman. She was one of a kind. The thought left me shaken. How was it that I could touch Izzy for a few minutes without harm, like I had a year ago in Penelopee's elevator? What was it about her? Or was it something with me? Something to do with my curse?

Fuck the danger. I would fight till the bitter end to learn the truth. I would never give up.

Not when the cost was so great.

I glanced at Izzy, who was slowly gaining her feet, and then at the pile of Post-it notes littering the floor. I knelt down and went back to work, more determined than ever to find my parents and the cure for my electrical curse.

"Blue," Izzy said once she regained her senses. I didn't look up from the paper in my hand. "Blue," she said again, louder. I continued to ignore her. What was there to say? Until I found a cure, I had nothing to offer, unlike Clark Boyer or other normal guys. Izzy deserved more than a few fumbling minutes once a year.

She deserved better than the likes of me.

"Fine," she said after a few minutes of silence. "I'm going to give Right and Left the rest of the night off and then I'm going to bed. I assume you're sleeping on the couch?" She paused, the husky spoken offer nearly my undoing. When I didn't react, she slowly nodded, walking to my bedroom door–like curtain. "I guess that's it, then."

And it was, as she pushed the curtain aside with more force than necessary and disappeared inside. I watched her walk away through veiled eyes, the burning in my chest unabated. With renewed passion I returned to my quest.

CHAPTER 44

In the wee hours of the night I found what I was looking for. Oddly enough it wasn't inside the stack of Post-it notes, but a paper clinging to the side of the box. I'd been at my wits' end, and then I'd noticed the white edge of the paper between the flaps of the cardboard box. I'd pulled the paper free, my eyes rounding when I realized what I held in my hands. A final bill from Shady Wings Nursing Home. My find had so excited me, the edge of the paper where my fingers gripped began to burn. I quickly blew the smoldering paper out.

I picked up my phone and dialed.

Alice's sleepy voice answered on the fourth ring. "What?"

"It's Blue."

"I don't care what color it is, you freak." And she hung up the phone.

I waited, counting off the seconds. My phone rang three minutes and thirty-four seconds later. I answered sweetly. "Hello?"

"Um, hi," Alice said, her voice husky. "Sorry about that. I was asleep . . ."

"No problem," I said enjoying her discomfort. "I have a job for you."

"Okay," she said slowly, as if weighing my mental status. Not that I blamed her. The last time we'd talked I'd nearly burned up the entire office. "What do you need?"

I quickly filled her in on what I'd found. She listened while I explained what I wanted her to do, only interrupting to ask one question. "I'm getting paid double time for this, right?"

I grinned. "Consider it hazard pay."

With that she hung up the phone and went to work.

I, on the other hand, spread out on my cramped couch, my feet hanging over the edge. I shifted to my side, my gaze falling on the lone figure lying behind the curtain in my bed, her wings rising and falling as she slept the sleep of angels. I watched her until my eyes finally grew heavy and I fell into a dreamless sleep.

Three hours later Izzy poked me awake with the end of a rolled-up magazine. I groaned once, slowly cracking my sandman-riddled eyelids open. I ran my tongue over my teeth, thirty-one in total. A habit I had yet to break. It came from spending too much time around fairies.

Izzy apparently noticed, for she smacked me in the head with the magazine and walked away with a softly spoken threat. "If I wanted your teeth, I'd take them. Anytime. Anywhere. Count on it."

I rolled to a sitting position and grinned, feeling better than I had in a week, even on less than three hours of sleep. Today I would find the man and woman behind the machine. I just knew it. In celebration only, I added a good amount of Irish to my morning coffee, the burn of which eased some of the burning still left in my loins after last night's amorous debacle.

My phone rang shortly after I finished the very last drop of spiked coffee. I picked it up, glanced at the caller ID, and pressed the talk button. "You got something?" I asked, a little surprised since I'd given Alice the task only three hours ago.

"It's why you pay me the less-than-big-but-better-than-eating-cat-food bucks," she answered smartly. She sounded like she needed a nap, which made me smile. "The address you gave me off the Shady Wings bill came back to a holding company."

I bit my lip, my good mood slowly fading. I'd thought for sure the bill would lead to my parents. How else would a woman with no family or money to speak of live her last days in a private-care nursing home? Most in Christine's situation ended up in a state-run facility wearing ratty bathrobes and smelling like week-old diapers. So either Christine had stocked away all her Tooth Fairy cash along with every penny she ever made or someone else was footing the bill. But why? What was it exactly that Christine had known?

Alice wasn't finished. "I hacked the New Never City assessor's records and found the names of the officers of the holding company."

Goody, I thought but didn't voice my sarcasm.

"One name popped out at me during the search."

"Yeah?" I gripped the phone tighter, half expecting to hear the name Smith.

"James W. Jones."

"The *W* stand for 'Wild' by any chance? As in our intern James Wild?"

"Oh, yes."

I let out a laugh. "Nice job. I'll see you at the office in a couple of hours."

"Okay . . . but . . . ," she said with a tension-filled pause.

"What?"

The pause grew longer. "This could very well be a trap."

I cracked my knuckles in anticipation, my pulse buzzing with electrical current. "I sincerely hope so."

CHAPTER 45

An hour later I stood outside the high-rise of James Wild's last known residence. His real residence, not the one I'd visited a few days ago. The one Alice had uncovered during a search of New Never City records. Records I would've never been able to access on my own. Computer-savvy investigators had really put a damper on the leg-breaking aspects of the business.

Man, how I longed for the good old days.

Much to my disgust, James owned a loft in the heart of the city, a place where you had to wipe your feet before walking on the street, let alone the sidewalk. The rent in the city was astronomical. I could only imagine what the price of a loft in a swanky high-rise would be.

Not that I'd ever want to live there. I liked my run-down apartment in my less-than-desirable neighborhood. What it lacked in physical safety it more than made up for in fairy-dust-addicted hookers and the sweet smell of spray paint in the morning.

I fingered the lock picks in my jacket, sneaking a glance at Izzy. She stood a little behind me in a tight black dress, her wings invisible and a set of diamonds around her neck. The dress was hers. She kept it at the office for just such an emergency. The diamonds we'd borrowed from one of our more notorious clients. They belonged to his mistress, and if we didn't return them in their original pristine condition, I wouldn't have to worry about some faceless killer anymore.

Risking my life for a valuable set of baubles didn't worry me overmuch. Not nearly as much as having Izzy watching my back. I wanted her as far away from danger as she could get. But she had other ideas. Mainly she wouldn't listen to a word I said, nor would she let me leave the apartment without her and her fairyguards, who stood silently judging me. Even though I tried. I'd even gone as far as electrocuting the doorknob. Much to my dismay, they'd used the fire escape. But if things went bad, those two might be useful.

"I go in and you wait here until I give the all clear," I said to Izzy. Right and Left had agreed to stay there, ensuring no one arrived for a sneak attack. Izzy agreed with a nod to stay put until I ushered her forward, though I doubted her sincerity.

I adjusted the silk tie around my neck, ducking inside the high-rise where James had lived. Surprisingly the doorman held the door wide, truly a miracle given the electric-blue hue of my hair. I was surprised he didn't immediately call the cops. I looked like a thug, no matter how shiny my loafers. And the doorman knew it. You could put lipstick on each of the three little pigs, but those pre–pork rinds would still bite.

Then again, who really questioned a man in a three-thousand-dollar suit?

Not to mention one with the power to burn the place to the ground with a flick of the wrist. I motioned Izzy to follow, which she did, stumbling twice on the four-inch heels two sizes too big she had borrowed from Doreen, the bitchy receptionist.

The second time she stumbled, the doorman caught her before she hit the floor, and she shot him a thankful smile, fluttering her eyelashes as she did so. I rolled my eyes. When would she learn not to overplay her hand? Though I saw through her innocent act, her awkwardness worked like a charm on the guards. Like his partner, the guy with the gun on his hip manning the security desk fell for it too, waving us through without question.

I guess there was something to say for having Izzy along for a little B and E.

Without a word we boarded the elevator with access from the parking garage below to the penthouse suit. The only problem was you needed an electronic key card to go anywhere. A key card I didn't possess. Damn secure buildings. It made one want to steal something just for the hell of it.

"Shit," I said quietly. We needed to search the loft, and we needed to do it soon, before this building "accidently" caught fire as well. I scratched the blue hairs on my chin, thinking. I could probably shock the guard into giving up his key card, but that would draw too much attention. I wanted time to thoroughly search the loft without being interrupted by half a dozen armed cops. The NNPD tended to frown on any illegal activity around here. Go figure.

"What's wrong?" Izzy asked, patting the blond wing she wore over her fiery-red hair. "We're inside like you wanted."

I motioned to the control panel on the elevator. "We need a key card, and unless you have one hidden in that dress"—a fact I doubted since it barely contained Izzy—"we're screwed."

She reached in the dress, down between her breasts, and pulled a card no bigger than a driver's license from her cleavage. I did my best not to look, though I might've glimpsed a bit of boob before she covered up. "Voilà," she said, holding out the card.

"How'd you . . ." I grabbed the slightly heated card from her hand.

"I picked the doorman's pocket." Izzy smiled, shifting her breasts back into the confines of the much-too-tight dress. "I took a class on pickpocketing a few months ago." She grinned. "At the adult annex. They teach everything at the annex."

Damn, I guess they did.

"This summer I'm going to learn how to white-water raft." She smiled. "A girl's got to keep her options open."

Not nearly as useful as pickpocketing considering we didn't live within four hours of a drop of white water. Putrid green and smelling of dead dwarf mobsters was more New Never City's style. But I just nodded, wanting to stay on Izzy's good side. Who knew what else they taught at the adult annex?

The elevator began to rise once I slipped in the key card and pressed the button for the thirty-fourth floor. I counted off the numbers as we rose into the sky, wondering what sort of secrets my former intern's loft would reveal. It was hard to think of James as anything more than a kid who brought me coffee and checked my mail. But he was more.

Much more.

Now I just had to figure out who'd pulled his strings.

CHAPTER 46

As the numbers whizzed by on the elevator console I considered the evidence against James. As thin as it was, I knew it was true. He'd used Izzy's key to enter my apartment, supposedly to bring my tuxedo home, but he had a very different mission in mind. Had he not accidently dropped the bottle of water into the rock-salt-and-electricity mixture, I would've walked right into a death trap.

Smart plan overall, as long as one didn't possess butterfingers. I smiled, which quickly turned to a frown when I considered the very real possibility that we might be walking into another trap. Were my parents waiting for their electrified offspring a few floors above? A part of me hoped so. Then, out of the corner of my eye, I saw Izzy biting her bottom lip.

I slammed my hand against the stop button on the console. The elevator jolted to a halt, knocking us both forward. I steadied myself against the doors, but Izzy wasn't so lucky. Already unsteady on her borrowed heels, she stumbled, crashing to the floor. I reached out to steady her but only ended up shocking her instead. Once the Taser-like effect wore off, Izzy raised an eyebrow in question. I winced. "Sorry about that."

"Why did you stop the elevator?" she asked as she stumbled to her feet, brushing at the dress clinging to her every curve.

I shot her a guilty smile. "I was trying to protect you."

She gazed down at the scorch marks on her arm where I'd tried to steady her. "Is that so?"

I shrugged. "Anyway . . ."

"No," she responded in a cold, curt tone. "I am not about to let you walk into what could very well be a trap without backup." She paused, her eyes boring into mine. "We're partners, Blue. For better and worse."

I raised a blue eyebrow. "Till death do we part. I don't think so. This is my fight. Not yours."

Instead of getting angry like I expected, Izzy let out a loud laugh. "This is a Reynolds & Davis fight. If you remember correctly, I hired that killer intern, and I'll be damned if I let you play hero while I am relegated to dim-witted damsel."

"But—"

"Forget it," she said, slamming her hand against the stop control. The elevator jerked again in response, once again rising into the sky. I closed my eyes, praying I wouldn't live to regret the next few minutes.

When the elevator quietly slid to a stop, I prepared myself, my body buzzing with electricity. Izzy stood a foot behind me. I could feel her body tense as the doors glided open.

I took a calming breath and then stepped forward into a killer's domain.

When nothing immediately killed me, much to my surprise and relief, I took yet another step inside. And another. And another. Still breathing, I moved deeper into the loft. At my signal Izzy slowly followed. The only sound in the loft besides the crackle of electrical current sparking through me was the clicking of her heels on the hardwood floor. I held up my hand for her to stop when we approached a closed door, a door that turned out to lead into a bathroom the size of the puddle left following the giant's fall from the beanstalk after Jack bungled the giant's palace.

Since nothing appeared wanting to do us harm in the tub, I closed the door once more, continuing the room-by-room search. Pretty easy, considering that the loft, while huge, was basically one large space with a bathroom off to the side. A bed the size of the most jovial of giants sat up against one wall. The bedsheets were crumpled, both pillows dented. James hadn't spent his last night on earth alone.

Sadly it wasn't some brilliant investigational prowess that led me to that conclusion, but the used condom I'd noticed in the bathroom trash. So where was this clandestine crumpet? I peered closer at the pillows, noting a long, shiny golden hair trapped in the fabric. It shone like a diamond, all but screaming the word "clue." I frowned, considering the long blond strand.

Since I didn't see any knickknacks or lacy crap everywhere, I doubted James's companion spent much time at the loft. Which made me wonder how well she had known him. Did she know he was a hired killer? Did she care? Women, I'd learned long ago, could forgive and forget many things, especially when a guy owned a loft this size. I inhaled deeply, nearly gagging as stale air filled my lungs. By the smell, it was obvious that no one, including the blonde, had been inside this loft for a few days. Izzy echoed my words a short time later. "No one lives here," she said. "Not anymore."

I nodded. "James did, though."

"How do you know?"

I pointed to the desk in the far corner of the loft. It looked out over the city like a king over his less-than-noble subjects. But it was the stack of papers piled atop that drew my notice. "The kid never could keep his desk straight."

Izzy let out a laugh, her eyes alight with relief. "I doubt we'll find anything useful in that mess."

But I just shook my head, crossing the room to the messy desk without another word. Investigators thrived on chaos, on mess. It was how we solved cases. James hadn't expected to die that day at my apartment, and unless his cohorts in crime or the blonde had cleaned up—and it didn't look like anyone had—there would be a clue among the clutter. I just had to separate evidence from . . . I frowned as I pulled a two-week-old éclair from the mess. But my point was the same.

The simple lack of clutter in the room at the frat house had been my first clue that there was more to James Wild than what I knew. I hadn't realized the significance then, but it shone like a neon sign now. People were messy by nature. We left a trail behind wherever we went. James Wild was no different. He would lead me to the answers I sought.

I opened the top drawer of his desk, taking a quick inventory. Nothing much of interest grabbed my attention. Paper clips, rubber bands, a few wayward staples stuck to the bottom of the mostly bare cupboard. I closed that drawer and opened the next. Still nothing except copies of invoices from the Shady Wings Nursing Home. I was right about James paying Christine's bills in order to keep her silence, but not for the reason I first suspected. I had a feeling James had kept Christine's location a secret from my parents as some sort of leverage. It was something I would've done in his shoes. Maybe the kid had learned something from me after all.

The guilt I felt over Christine's death intensified. Had I not found her, maybe they never would've either. Maybe Christine would still be alive and safe. Izzy's cell phone buzzed, tearing me from my dark thoughts. She silenced it with a stab of her finger.

Damn. How could I have missed it? Whoever had hired James to kill me had to contact him somehow, which meant there would be a trail. How I loved a trail, especially one that an idiot could follow. I pulled out my cell phone, dialing quickly.

Izzy nodded at the phone in my hand. "Who are you calling?"

"Alice," I mouthed to Izzy when my sleep-deprived employee answered. "I need you to run a search for any e-mail addresses or phones listed to James or his phony corporation." I paused to listen while Alice worked her magic. The sound of her fingers across the keyboard was much like the furious pounding of a hare at the start of a footrace.

"Okay," she said half a minute later. "Sorry, boss, but no dice. No phones registered to James, let alone paid for with any of his credit cards. And I don't remember ever seeing him with one, which is weird, since even a guy like you has a—"

"Watch it."

"Right," she said. "I couldn't find any e-mail addresses either, other than our company one."

Damn. "Okay, thanks," I said, hanging up with a frown. How was that possible? James had to be in contact with my parents somehow. Was Alice wrong? I quickly shook off that thought. Alice's computer searches were never wrong. I turned to Izzy. "Looks like this trip was a waste of time." From the grin on Izzy's face, I guessed she didn't agree. "What?" I asked.

"What?"

I shook my head. "Don't play with me, Isabella. You are keeping something from me."

"I keep a lot of things from you."

I took a menacing step forward. "Like what?"

"Relax," she said quickly. "I'm kidding." Even though she had sounded damn sincere. Add in our past history and I'd be a fool to believe her. Then again, things were different now. We were partners. "Blue," she began. "What happened to James's cell phone?"

"What?"

"His phone." She ran her index finger over her bottom lip. "He had a cell phone the day he went to your apartment. I remember it ringing as I handed him my key to your place." She gave a slight wince. "Again, sorry about that."

I rolled my eyes. "Alice said he didn't own a phone. At least not one registered to him. And he wasn't paying a mobile bill either."

She shook her head. "What if he had a secret burner phone? You know the kind most of our cheating spouses invest in?"

"You're right." I clapped my hands together with excitement. A rainbow of sparks floated down, leaving tiny scorch marks on the hardwood. Not that James would notice or care. Being dead seemed to have that effect on people.

"So where is it?" Izzy asked, biting her lip as she surveyed the loft.

"I know exactly where it is." A slow smile spread across my mouth. Finding it would probably cost me no more than a box of jelly dough-nuts, but it would be well worth it in the end.

Or did cops prefer sprinkles?

CHAPTER 47

Izzy stood next to me as we gazed up at the imposing building in front of us. The New Never City police headquarters was a structure built sometime around the turn of the century, a few centuries ago. It was a stone fortress, cold and foreboding, the perfect place to sweat a criminal or upstanding citizen like yours bluely. I'd spent more than a few nights locked in an interrogation room inside. And then a few more locked in a cell in the dungeon below. I wasn't sure which was worse.

Today I had a very different reason for being here—solving a crime rather than lying about committing one. Oddly enough, they felt very much the same. Though, if I was honest, I preferred the former. Asking a cop for anything went against my thuggish code. But James's burner cell phone could be the key to everything.

Or it could be a complete waste of time.

One more dead end in a long list of them.

Steeling myself, I started up the steps, what felt like a couple of thousand of them to a smoker like me. Izzy was already at the top when I finally wheezed my way up, gasping. I stopped to catch my breath. She glared at me. "Smoking will kill you."

"I'll risk it," I wheezed to annoy her. Pressing my hand to my left side, I added, "Besides, I'm sure my liver will give up long before my lungs."

"Your liver is on the right." She shook her head sadly. "Remind me to up your life insurance."

I snorted, switching my hand to the right side of my body. "Like I would make you my beneficiary."

She gave a snort of her own. "Like I can't forge your signature."

"They teach that at the adult annex too?"

Rather than answer she shot me a wicked smile, turned on her heel, and disappeared inside the New Never City Police Plaza, leaving me wheezing on the steps, wondering just how much life insurance she had on me. I had a feeling I wouldn't like the answer.

"What do you want, Reynolds?" Detective Peter Rabit asked with a weary sigh. His hundred-dollar suit was rumpled, as if he'd slept in it. But that didn't stop him from leering at the fairy next to me when he finally looked up long enough to notice her. Hell, I half expected him to start drooling, and not from the box of bribery-coated doughnuts in my gloved hand.

I pushed the box at Rabit. "These are for you." I lowered my voice to add, "She is not. Got it?"

He took the box, but his eyes stayed firmly on Izzy. "I'm busy, so make it quick."

"I need to see James Wild's personal effects."

He snorted. "For what?"

"Closure?"

His next snort was louder.

"Fine," I said, taking out my wallet and passing him a hundred bucks. "Let's call it a professional courtesy."

Rabit shook his head, but his nondescript, overly gelled hair didn't move an inch. "Add another hundred and we'll call it good."

Annoyed but willing to do anything—I glanced at Rabit and his leering gaze—or almost anything to get the burner phone, I pulled out another hundred and slapped it on the desktop. Cops today. A few years ago a hundred bucks would've bought me a baggie of personal effects as well as a few baggies of fairy dust. When his hand went for the cash, I smashed my hand on top of it. "Effects first."

He rolled his eyes but headed toward the evidence room just the same. I looked at Izzy, her wings brightly colored against the backdrop of the institutionally grey walls, and felt instantly better. It was nice to have her watching my back, though I would never admit it. Not for a second. I'd eat a blind mouse first.

As I was finishing my girlish musings Rabit returned, a thick padded envelope in his hand. He ripped the seal and emptied the contents onto the desk in front of us. Sure enough a cell phone dropped onto the desktop, as did a wallet and a driver's license in the name of James W. Jones. No wonder James had used the name Wild. After all, the surname Jones didn't inspire confidence when hiring a killer. Not that Wild was much better.

I reached for the cell phone but Rabit grabbed my gloved hand before I touched it. "You can look, but no touching," he said. I raised an eyebrow but didn't argue. Cops had a thing about chain of custody. Not like thugs. We just had a thing for chains. "Did you trace his last call?" I asked.

Rabit laughed without humor. "Are you telling me how to do my job, PI?"

"Of course not," I said. "I was asking. That's all."

He rolled his eyes. "I suggest you ask somewhere else before my good mood vanishes and your ass ends up in the holding cells." He paused, his eyes roaming over Izzy's body, stopping on her wings. "You, I'll keep right here."

She smiled, stepping around me to flirt with the dickhead of a detective. "Is that so? What will you do with me?"

I turned away, the urge to fry Rabit nearly overwhelming. Taking gulping breaths, I tried to calm the desire. The leather of my shoe started to smolder. The cop seated at a desk a few feet away, jelly doughnut puffing out his cheeks like a hamster, glanced up. "We grilling burgers for lunch?"

I stomped the smoking shoe out, returning my attention to Izzy, who was now practically sitting in Rabit's lap. What the hell was she thinking? He was an even worse choice than our VP Clark. Hell, the guy smelled of cheap aftershave and hookers. When I couldn't stomach a minute more, I grabbed Izzy's arm in my gloved hand. "Time to go."

She didn't argue, taking her time to scramble off Rabit. She shot him a large, toothy grin. He returned her smile. "Call me," he said, winking as he tucked his card into the crease between her wings and shoulder blade. She winked back.

I pulled her toward the door, thankful when we reached the exit without my being arrested or electrocuting a certain detective. Once we were outside in the crisp afternoon air, Izzy gave a shudder. "I need a shower. Maybe two of them."

"What?"

"You're kidding, right?" Her tone conveyed just what she thought of me. "You really believed I was into that guy? Give me some credit, Blue."

"Then . . ." I glanced down at her hand. "You stole the cell phone."

"I'm getting pretty damn good at this petty-crime thing."

I took the phone from her. "Sorry to be the one to break this to you, but stealing evidence from the cop shop is a little more than a petty crime." I paused, my eyes burning with electricity.

Izzy swallowed, stepping back a small step. "Blue . . . we . . ."

I shook off the desire to kiss her until she moaned. "Right. The case." I blew out a harsh breath. "We should go back to the office, give the phone to Alice, and see if she can prove my parents hired James to kill me."

I spun on my heel and started down the stairs, nearly missing Izzy's softly spoken words. "The case always comes first." Her words were far from comforting.

CHAPTER 48

Following our mini crime spree at the police plaza, we grabbed a taxi and set off for Reynolds & Davis. Right and Left followed behind in a second cab, leaving Izzy and me alone for a few minutes. My heart pulsed in my chest with unquenched lust and a renewed sense of purpose. James's cell phone was just what I needed to crack this case. I could feel it.

I glanced over at my pink-winged obsession, smiling as she juggled her cell phone and her iPad. Izzy wasn't one to let a minute go by without making the most of it. I, on the other hand, let too many minutes and opportunities go by. Most times it was easier that way. Less mess. No fuss. "Is Alice in?" she was asking whoever was on the other line. "Doreen, tell her to stay there. We'll be right in."

She hung up and smiled. "Alice is at her desk."

"Excellent." I fingered James's cell phone. As soon as the taxi pulled to a stop in front of our offices, I tossed a few bucks at the cabbie and leapt from the cab. The doorman barely had time to reach for the handle of the door before I ripped it open and plowed my way inside. Izzy followed on my heels, or rather her heels, teetering with each step. Finally she apparently had enough, kicked off her offending footwear, and ran after me. I stabbed the elevator call button.

"Blue," Izzy said, reaching for my gloved hand but pulling away before making contact. "Maybe we should just drop this, forget about James and your past . . ."

"What? Why?" I asked, surprised. When she didn't answer I shook my head. "Izzy, you know me. You know what this means to me. What it could mean for me." I nodded to my vibrating fingers. "Why would I stop before I learn the truth?"

Her eyes met mine, and I swore I saw tears well in them. "Because it won't set you free, Blue."

My forehead wrinkled. "What's that mean?"

She blinked a few times, and the wetness disappeared. A trick of the light, I told myself, though I knew better. Izzy was keeping something from me, something that could very well destroy our tenuous partnership, let alone whatever sort of other relationship we had. Rather than continue our current conversation, I cowardly turned to the open elevator doors, motioning her inside.

I followed Izzy into the elevator with her warning rushing through my head. As we rose from floor to floor, my fear twisted to anger, and electrical current started to buzz through me, rising as we did. Growing hotter and hotter until I lost all control.

Izzy jumped back just in time, her wings only slightly singed. "Stop," she ordered, but I couldn't hear her over the snap, crackle, and buzzing in my brain. For a few brief moments, I was a god, an angry and vengeful one, sure, but godlike nonetheless.

And then Izzy's hand touched my shoulder.

But rather than causing her to be knocked across the elevator by the sheer power I was emitting, her touch had the opposite effect. I winked out. I wasn't sure what she'd done, or why it happened, but the current was gone. I staggered against the wall, using my hands to steady me. Before I could speak, to let forth the flurry of accusations inside my head, the elevator dinged, announcing our arrival.

I swallowed back every dark word, focusing on what was important, or at least what I could actually fix. The case. I could and would solve this case. My fingers tightened on the cell phone, the plastic smooth against the leather of my gloves.

"Blue," Izzy said. "For what it's worth . . . I am sorry."

I nodded, unable to look at her, and then exited the elevator, one goal in mind as I headed off to find my bespectacled employee Alice. Thankfully she was right where she always was, though she wasn't quite the eager, annoyingly willing to please investigator she normally was, especially when I pulled to a stop in front of her desk. "Blue," she said, pushing her glasses up her nose with her index finger, hiding the dark circles around her eyes. "Do you need something?"

"I need you to run a search on this phone," I said, running my finger across the screen, surprised to see it flicker to life. Some investigator I was. I hadn't even checked to see if it was locked. I blamed Izzy. She was too much of a distraction. I'd be better off on my own, I told myself, even though I knew it was a lie. Izzy had saved me from destitution, but also from myself. Left to my own devices, I would be dead by forty. With her around I had a few more years, as long as the life insurance policy didn't become too tempting.

Izzy arrived behind me as I swiped my fingers over the touch screen, searching for the very last number dialed. I smiled when the New Never City area code appeared on-screen. Thankfully I didn't recognize the phone number.

"Blue, wait—" Alice said as I pressed the send button for the last number dialed.

A resulting ringing burst forth.

But not from the phone in my hand.

CHAPTER 49

The phone rang again. Izzy and I glanced down. Alice looked up, her eyes growing three times bigger under the lenses of her glasses. I shoved her back with a gloved hand, ripping open her desk drawer with the other. Inside sat an old-style flip phone, a burner phone like James's that was lighting up like a Christmas tree as it rang unabated.

Alice made a move for the ringing phone, but I stopped her before her fingers reached it. My hand gripped her delicate skin, leaving red glove prints along her forearm. "I swear," she said, her voice choked, "I've never seen that phone before."

"Now, why don't I believe that?" I said, keeping Alice back with one hand while I pulled out the burner phone with my other. I tossed the phone to Izzy, who much to my pleasure caught it with one hand. "Why don't you and I have a little talk?" I said to Alice, helping her from her seat without ever breaking contact between us.

"Use my office," Izzy said, waving us forward.

"Please," Alice cried. "I don't understand any of this."

Ignoring her plea, I maneuvered her through our busy office, past Doreen, the bitchy receptionist, toward Izzy's office. Doreen sneered with disgust as we moved by, and for once we were on the same page. I thought of the blond hair on the pillow at James's loft. It was Alice's. It had to be. She was probably the one behind the mechanical call to Bo Peep, as well as the fires, while all the while looking as pure and innocent as freshly fallen snow. I'd never suspected a thing. I'd trusted her and she'd betrayed me. I was a fool.

I couldn't begin to understand the ramifications of her betrayal. Yet one question kept repeating inside my head: Why? Once I had her locked inside Izzy's office, I asked her as much. "What's this all about, Alice? What do you have against me?"

But Alice had stopped talking. She just sat in her chair, her eyes as clear as day behind her thick lenses. I decided on another tactic. With great effort, my tone lost its hard edge, and I sat down across from her. "It's okay," I began. "I get it."

"Get what?" She blinked like an owl.

I smiled kindly. Or at least as kindly as I could. I knew my grin had missed its mark when she flinched. "You and James," I said, thinking back to the photograph I'd stolen from James's frat-house room. A picture of a younger version of Alice.

How could I have missed it?

In my defense, the image was grainy and most of the woman's face was obscured by sun glare, but it was Alice. I was 80 percent sure of it. Ninety-five when I factored in the blond hair on the pillow. She was James's lover.

But was she also a killer?

CHAPTER 50

An hour later, exhausted and numb, I watched as Jonas and another security guard marched Alice from Izzy's office. I felt nothing as I watched the trio disappear into the elevator. Izzy was waiting for me as I stepped out of her office, a crystal tumbler of whiskey in her hands. I took it and swallowed the burning liquor in one gulp.

"Hey," she complained. "I was drinking that."

"Not fast enough," I countered. "Izzy, I think it's time we—"

Clark popped his head out of his office, cutting me off. "I still can't believe it," he said. "Not one, but two employees plotting to kill you. It boggles the mind."

Izzy smiled. "Not after you spend enough time with Blue. I'm actually surprised it took someone this long."

"Funny," I said, thinking it was anything but; in fact, a part of me took my employees' betrayal very personally. I vowed that the next time we hired anyone, they'd have to sign a waiver promising not to attempt to murder me no matter how much they'd like to. I suspected Izzy might balk at the idea, but I was pretty sure she'd come around.

Eventually.

Which was why I didn't immediately fill her in on my plan.

I had one. No doubt about it.

Whether it would work was a whole different story.

Izzy snapped her fingers in front of my face to gain my attention. "Blue," she said sharply, "Clark asked you a question."

"Oh." I blinked a few times. "What's up?"

Ever the gracious gentleman, Clark smiled brightly. His smile had to be fake. His teeth were too straight and white to be anything but veneers. Probably ones he'd had since birth. "I asked if you'd like to join Isabella and myself for dinner." He paused as his eye roamed over my expensive suit, but it wasn't nearly as ritzy as his own. "We'll go somewhere more casual. Unless you'd like to change?"

I shook my head, suddenly beyond tired. "I'll pass." Though it killed me, I added, "You two have fun, though." What I really wanted to say was, I hope you die of food poisoning, Clark. I instantly felt bad for my dark thoughts. Clark was an okay guy.

Hell, I still hoped a mild case of VD on him.

"If you're sure?" Izzy asked, her eyes filled with concern.

I nodded.

She leaned in, her lips ever so slightly brushing my cheek. A spark shot between us, but she didn't move away. "Good night, Blue," she said. "I'll see you later."

A chill puckered my flesh like an omen at her softly spoken words.

A cold drizzle fell from the sky, soaking through my suit jacket. I shivered, pulling the collar against the back of my neck, both to keep the rain out and to keep Right and Left from realizing they'd been ditched again. Whatever Izzy was paying them was obviously too much if they couldn't keep their target in sight. I grinned as I slipped past Right without a second glance.

Two blocks up, I searched the shadows for a dark-colored sedan parked at the curb. Peyton had left it for me after I called him a few hours ago. I had no idea where he'd gotten it, nor did I really care. I had more important things on my mind.

I made my way to the car, a smile lining my face when the driver's side door offered no resistance. I ducked inside, nearly breaking my leg, as the seat was less than a foot from the dashboard. "Damn it," I yelped, throwing the seat back so it fit my six-foot frame.

Once I was finally settled, I started the engine and pulled into traffic, narrowly avoiding a passing ice cream truck. I slammed on the brakes in time, but my heart continued to pound in my chest for the rest of the trip to Alphabet Soup City.

As I crossed the bridge into the land of Avenues A, B, and C, the gentle aromas of tomatoes and broth tickled my nostrils. Not unpleasant, but it did make me hungry. Over the growling of my stomach, I lit a cigarette, a sad replacement for a four-course meal, but it would have to do. It would be a long time before I enjoyed more than a stale bag of chips.

I thought of Izzy and Clark seated in some fancy restaurant, waiters hovering to anticipate their every need while mounds of delicious food were piled on the table. Tonight Clark would make his move. He'd say something witty and Izzy would laugh, letting her guard down. Clark would press his advantage, pouring her more and more wine, until her defenses were completely down and she was his for the taking.

The very thought killed my growing appetite. My hands tightened on the wheel until the woven pattern on the steering wheel cover was etched into the leather of my gloves. I took a deep breath, relaxing my grip.

Since I didn't have a license, I stayed well below the speed limit, my phone giving me vague directions to my final destination in a snobby tone. Half an hour later I pulled to the curb and parked. The windshield wipers screeched across the pitted windshield, so I turned them off before the sound drew attention to the guy in the driver's seat.

I hunkered down in my seat, my breathing the only sound. Apparently people other than old men with large bumps on their heads had a dislike for the soggy weather. The normally packed streets were empty. The red, yellow, and green of the stoplights reflected in the rain puddles, pulling me into a hypnotic trance. I blinked a few times, trying to keep from falling asleep.

Hell, I'd been waiting for only twenty minutes.

With a yawn, I rubbed the growth of blue whiskers on my chin as I counted up to a thousand and back down again, by sevens, to keep awake. A feat a hell of a lot harder than it sounded. The passenger side door of the car opened, sending a swift, cold burst of air around me. I glanced up. "Took you long enough," I complained to the woman now seated next to me.

Alice pushed the rim of her glasses up her nose with her middle finger but didn't comment. Instead she tossed a stack of files in my lap. I gazed down at the top file, Izzy's name emblazoned across the top. "Any trouble getting them?" I asked.

She shook her head, her eyes fixed on the rain-streaked window for a full minute. "I wanted to thank you."

I frowned. "For what?"

She swallowed. "For believing me this afternoon. Believing I wasn't in cahoots with James, even though you found that phone in my desk."

I shrugged. It hadn't been hard to believe in her innocence. It took me about ten minutes to realize the truth. Alice had been framed. While exceedingly accident-prone, she was far from stupid. So why would she leave evidence of her crimes in her own desk? I suspected someone had planted the burner phone and the blond hair on the pillow at the loft, not to mention the picture of the obscured blonde at the frat house.

Which meant one thing: James did have a partner.

And he or she was just the lead I needed to find my parents.

James's partner must've overheard me tell Izzy about the Ferns' claim of having seen a woman with hair as blond as spun gold and decided to pin everything on Alice. I had little doubt of her innocence given her IQ, which was why I'd arranged for her very public exit. I wanted whoever had planted the bogus evidence to feel safe.

From the looks on everyone's faces as Alice was dragged from the building by Jonas and his security guard pal, my plan had worked perfectly. Now it was time to catch a killer, or rather a few killers, two of whom were also known as Mom and Dad.

CHAPTER 51

When we'd found the burner phone in Alice's drawer, it had taken me less than ten minutes to put two and two together and come up with a few suspects. Considering the only people with access to Alice's desk were employees of Reynolds & Davis Securities, my suspect pool was fewer than ten people total. I would find James's partner and that person would pay.

That was how I found myself sitting in a car in Alphabet Soup City with Alice in the passenger seat. I'd had her run the rest of the numbers called from James's phone, as well as the one we found in her desk this afternoon. She'd agreed to meet me far from the bright lights of our office when she had the information I needed.

According to Alice, the only other number found on James's burner phone was the Reynolds & Davis switchboard.

James's cohorts had been smart—never dialing him directly. Given that on an average day, we received and made more than five hundred phone calls at the office, tracking each call felt like an impossible task. And the killer knew it, too.

With that information swirling around my head, I had Alice pull every single employee's record, from the janitor to my partner. Somewhere there had to be some evidence of whom James had partnered with. An idea that quickly faded in the face of one fact—whoever had been working with James likely held a wee bit of a grudge after his death. I doubted they'd admit to anything, let alone starting two fires and murdering an old woman.

"The files have everything I could find on each name," Alice was saying. "Some more than others." She tapped Clark Boyer's file folder, which was as thick as a book, while her own was much slimmer. "I hope this helps."

I nodded, not quite sure what I expected to find. Picking up the first file, I ran my finger over Izzy's name. As much as I hated what I was about to do, I couldn't stop. Izzy had a secret, one she wasn't willing to share. And that put her in danger, especially if said secret had something to do with my past. As I flipped through the file, one piece of paper caught my eye. It was a list of computer searches, some seemingly innocent enough, but when they were viewed as a whole, a pattern emerged. I showed the list to Alice. "These are all from Izzy's computer?" I asked, the paper shaking along with my hand.

She nodded. "Mostly from three weeks ago. Nothing in the last week."

I closed my eyes, fear growing as the full weight of what I had read filled me.

I now knew what case Izzy had been working without me.

I just hoped it wouldn't take her from me too.

CHAPTER 52

While I waited for Izzy to arrive back at my apartment from her "date," I flipped through Clark's file without much interest. On paper Clark was the same as in person—completely vanilla—boring to the very end. The Boyer clan was a bit more interesting. Not enough to keep my mind from wandering, though.

I thought of what I would say to Izzy when she arrived home, if she came home tonight. That thought left me electrified with anger. I planned on slowly twisting the screws until she finally came clean, offering up all of her secrets like thousands had done for her with their molars. I blew on my heated fingertips as my attention returned to the Boyer file. The first family of New Never City. Hell, Clark's relatives had come over on the *Fairyflower*. Not a hint of scandal, let alone a gaggle full of murderous relations like yours bluely. The Boyers were New Never City élite, just as my former Tooth Fairy cohort was in Fairyland.

When, much to my disgust, my mind inadvertently pictured Izzy in Clark's arms, I tried to fight the feeling of inevitability. Two people of and from the same circles. Izzy might dabble on the dark side, but the cream always rose to the top.

And one day she'd leave me for, if not Clark, then someone very much like him.

The thought turned my stomach.

Suffice it to say I had worked myself into quite the rotten mood by the time Izzy arrived back at my place. I was half in the bag to boot. Whiskey had tasted a whole lot better than the half-eaten bag of chips I'd had for dinner when I returned home.

I sat in the dark, a half full bottle of whiskey in my hand, when Izzy unlocked my front door. I heard her say good night to Clark, thankful when she stepped inside alone a few seconds later. Keeping the lights off, she hurried by on her way to my bedroom. To my bed.

My grip tightened on the bottle, the cold smoothness doing nothing to ease the burning inside me. "Have a nice evening?" I asked from the shadows.

She gasped, dropping her purse. It hit the floor without a sound, the contents slipping out between us. A small, clear vial of dentin rolled in a circle, finally settling a few inches from my boot. My gaze stayed locked on the vial, too afraid to glance up at my partner. I was half afraid of what I might do when I did, but even more scared of what would happen if I chickened out and said nothing.

"Blue," Izzy said, a slight tremor in her tone. She took a small step forward, as if nothing was wrong when in truth everything we had was crashing in around us. "Is everything all right?"

Finally I glanced up, searching her beautiful yet treacherous face. She looked unsure and even a little afraid. "Don't lie to me." I slowly rose to face her, my legs as unsteady as my voice. "Not anymore, Izzy."

"I don't—"

"Yeah, you do, sweetheart." I licked my dry lips. "You've been investigating me for the past month."

CHAPTER 53

"I wanted to tell you," Izzy was saying as we stared at each other from what was only a few feet apart but might as well have been the length of an unspooled roll of floss. I lifted the whiskey bottle to my lips, drinking deeply to squelch the current threatening to rise. "But . . ." She trailed off.

"But what?" I swallowed past the lump of bitterness choking me. "You were what? Afraid of what I might do?"

She nodded slowly.

I laughed, loud and hollow. "You're lying, like you did every time I asked you about your case. How you must've laughed when I offered to help." Her lips thinned, but she didn't argue, though I wanted nothing more than a fight. "All this time my past was your super-secret case. To what end?"

She turned, giving me her back. "I never meant to hurt you. I was trying . . . I *am* trying to protect you."

"From what, Izzy? The truth? From freedom from this?" Electricity bolted from my fingers as my laughter grew darker. "Let me thank you for that. Really."

For the first time since she entered my apartment, genuine emotion showed through her façade, like ice cracking when electricity was applied. "You don't understand, Blue. There are things . . . secrets . . . about your parents."

I grabbed her arm, shocking us both literally and figuratively. I let go when sparks shot from my hand, burning her delicate skin. "You know where they are." I shoved my hands in my pockets to keep from throttling her. Didn't she see how dangerous the people who birthed me were? They'd already killed one person, and probably more, in hopes of hiding the very secrets Izzy now held. The thought of anyone, let alone the people who'd abandoned me, harming Izzy nearly drove me mad.

She took a few steps away, her eyes steady on the night sky beyond the grimy windows of my apartment. "Two months ago, completely by accident, mind you, I read the file you kept on your birth."

I snorted. "Considering it was locked in the bottom of my desk, I'm guessing the accident part is"—I paused—"like most of the things you say, a lie."

Her soft gasp told me I'd hit the mark. "Anyway," she said coldly, "I decided, as a friend, to do a little investigating on my own." I chuckled at her use of the word "friend," but let her continue her fairytale. "I didn't know what I would find, but I wanted to . . . thank you for giving me a chance to be something other than the expected." She emphasized her point by flapping her wings. A small cloud of fairy dust filled the air, taking some of the edge off my anger.

I inhaled deeply, hoping to ease the rest, including the gnawing fear churning in my gut. "I take it this is where I beg your forgiveness and tell you just how damn much I appreciate your attempt to help poor Little Boy Blue?"

Anger flashed across her face. "No need to be snarky. I admit my actions weren't the best, but my intentions were and are pure. I thought I was doing the right thing."

I gave a bitter laugh. "You want to do right by me? Then tell me where I can find them."

She closed her eyes. "I can't."

"Can't or won't?"

"You don't know what you're asking, Blue." A single tear slid down her cheek. "Please. Just let it go."

"Tell me," I barked. "Where are they?"

"The New Never City Cemetery."

CHAPTER 54

My parents were dead. Had been for quite some time. The headstones said so. Neatly engraved with the words "Husband" and "Wife," but no names accompanied them. I wondered why, but Izzy didn't have the answer and there was no one else left to ask.

The Wife headstone held a death date more than thirty years ago, right after my birth. My father had died five years later. Had he mourned her loss? Had the very thought of losing her choked him with sadness?

I glanced over at Izzy. She stood next to me, silent, watching the gravestones as if they held the answers to our tumultuous partnership. Surprisingly, her being by my side eased a little of the shock at the deaths of the people who'd borne me. Oddly that was all I felt. No grief or pain. Maybe that would come later. And maybe it wouldn't. After all, I'd never known either of them.

Were they good people?

Did it matter either way?

They were dead, buried in a mysterious cemetery open only twice a year, once in the spring and the other time in the fall. Unless you were fairy royalty; then you simply fluttered your wings at the gate-keeper and he let you and your glaring companion right in.

The cemetery was oddly beautiful, with marble headstones of the old city's elite. My parents were buried closer to the back, under a forest of trees, the perfect place to bury bodies—and their secrets. I wondered who'd done just that. Who had loved them enough to pay for their burials? Was it the same person willing to kill to keep their blue-haired secret?

"From what I learned, they loved each other very much," Izzy said quietly. "Your mother—her name was Cybil. She died with your father's name on her lips."

I turned away from her, not wanting to hear another word about the woman I would never know, the woman who gave me life. "How'd you find them?" When I couldn't, I added silently. Maybe this was meant to be, a way of showing me I wasn't quite the badass investigator I'd thought. Rather than humble me, Izzy's investigational prowess filled me with equal parts pride and self-disgust.

"I asked Christine."

I spun back toward Izzy. "What?"

"I asked Christine," she repeated, biting her bottom lip. "I somehow caught her in a moment of clarity, and she told me about Mr. and Mrs. Smith, about . . ."

"About what?"

"Their deaths."

"When?"

Her forehead wrinkled. "When did they die?"

I shook my head. "No. When did you go to see Christine?"

"You're not going to like my answer," she said.

"Try me," I said, though I had a strong feeling she was right.

Taking a few steps toward the graves, she ran her hand over the cold marble of my mother's headstone. "The day James was found at your apartment. I saw Christine that morning."

And James came to kill me that afternoon.

Too much of a coincidence to think there wasn't more to it.

Had Izzy's visit to Shady Wings started this mess? I didn't see how . . . unless someone at the home had notified James, the guy who paid the bills, of Izzy's visit and the questions she had asked. Or maybe he'd had a plant there all along? Just waiting for someone to show up and ask questions? I pictured the sweet fairy girl manning the reception desk. She'd known who Izzy was at first sight. Then again, the old bastard who'd cracked me in the knees with his cane seemed like a better suspect, mostly because of the three-inch-long bruise still imprinted on my leg.

I returned my attention to Izzy as she said, "I'd stumbled upon Christine by accident. I'd read your file, noticed the name, and remembered a visit to Shady Wings during my stint as the Tooth Fairy." She gave a small laugh. "I went to a lot of nursing homes. That and

Friday Night Gnome boxing tournaments are a Tooth Fairy's bread and butter."

"You remembered one old lady out of hundreds? How?"

She closed her eyes. "When I was at Shady Wings I said the word 'blue'—completely at random, mind you. Christine's eyes went wide and she started rambling about a fire and a baby boy named Blue." She paused as if gathering her thoughts. "I didn't mention it at the time because we . . . weren't on the best of terms."

I barked with bitter laughter. "Meaning you thought you could lord it over me."

"Maybe a little," she said, ducking her head. "But it didn't click in place until a few days ago. The next day I went to Shady Wings."

"That's why you wanted to go with me when Alice first found Christine. You wanted to keep me from the truth." I paused, waving a hand at the impersonal headstones. "From knowing they were dead."

She slowly shook her head. "Not that they were dead, exactly."

"Then what?"

Her eyes filled with tears. "To keep you from knowing how they died."

Months after my birth, by all accounts, my mother had died at my father's hands. He'd electrocuted her. The very same way I'd feared I would one day take someone's life. My father had then spent the next—and last—five years of his life locked in a prison cell.

I was far more like the man who gave me life than I'd known.

I prayed we wouldn't share the same fate.

CHAPTER 55

Hours after learning of my parents' deaths, I sat in my moldy office, reading and rereading the newspaper article about my mother's murder. The newspaper referred to them as a husband and wife from New Never City, never once mentioning their names.

Or the fact that they had a little blue-haired baby.

Was my mother's death the reason my father had dropped me on the doorstep of the orphanage? Was he horrified by what he'd done? I pictured Izzy's face, pale in death, and felt a lump rise in my throat. I now understood a little better why I'd been abandoned. Though I now had even less of a reason for James's attempting my murder and the two fires set to destroy the file. Both my parents were dead, so who was left to care about from the past?

Now that I was armed with the truth about my childhood, it was time to do a little digging into the night of my mother's murder. While I could've simply picked up the phone and delegated the duty to one of the other Reynolds & Davis investigators, I needed to do this myself.

As much as I hated to admit it, Izzy was right—the truth hadn't set me free as I'd believed it would. Instead I was left with myriad questions that I might never find the answers to. But foremost in my mind was the fact that I would never be normal. My father had gone to his deathbed an electrified monster. What made me think, even for a second, that I would avoid a similar fate? I just prayed Izzy wouldn't be the victim leading to my own murder trial. The thought left me cold.

I vowed, then and there, that whatever we were, once I found the person behind this, I would put as much distance as I could between us. Izzy would forever be safe from my electrified touch. My heart ached at the thought of leaving, but the risk was too great now that I knew the fairytale ending to my own parents' storybook marriage. The writing was plain to see. I would eventually lose whatever tiny bit of control I had over my power, and someone would die.

I pictured my mother, whose face I knew only from the faded newspaper article, and swallowed hard. Then I typed the date of my mother's death into the search engine on my computer and the name Cybil. Ten thousand results popped up, filling the screen with scenes of death, pain, and destruction from that date.

Just not any of the pain, death, or destruction I was looking for. "What the hell?" I asked the empty office. "The Net has pictures of fairy-on-gnome porn, yet they have nothing on a thirty-year-old murder."

Tapping a pencil against the desktop, I considered the ramifications of zero results. What did it mean? Was it possible I had the wrong name? Maybe I had the wrong date, I thought. But the newspaper article was dated the following day. A shiver ran up my spine. Was it possible for someone to hack the entire Internet, ridding the world of whatever secret he or she wanted to hide? With one small exception.

Me.

As the thought crossed my mind, my office door creaked open.

I turned toward the noise as a shot rang out.

CHAPTER 56

I awoke with a gasp, gulping large breaths of oxygen into my starved lungs. Thankfully the mask across my nose and mouth kept me from hyperventilating, though at the same time it added to my general anxiety. I blinked a few times and my eyes started to focus. White walls. White floors. White ceiling. Pink wings. The New Never City ER.

I ran my hands over my body, searching for new holes.

"Blue," Izzy yelled. "Stay still."

Rather than listen to what I'm sure was pretty good advice, I moved my hands up my face and then across my head, noting the gauzy covering on the top of my head. "What the hell happened?" I asked, ripping off the mask. I couldn't remember a damn thing that had happened past sitting in my office chair while I decided what my next move in the investigation should be.

"You were shot," Izzy said, her voice as sharp as nails on a chalkboard. "In the head."

I prodded the wound. "I'm guess it's just a flesh wound or you wouldn't be standing there glaring at me like it's my fault."

"I'd still be pissed, as you put it," she frowned, "but you'd be in a body bag."

Point taken. Someone had tried to kill me. Again. At this rate I was going to start taking these attempts to murder me personally. I guess Izzy was right, though. I really did have a hard head. I licked my dry lips, thankful to be alive. "Good thing we don't hire better shots."

"What?" she asked in a near shout. "You think someone at the office did this?"

Oops. Too late I remembered that I hadn't filled Izzy in on my latest pool of suspects. Hell, I hadn't even had the chance to tell her about Alice's innocence. "Um, Izzy . . . ," I began, and then told her about my suspicions. She watched me through veiled eyes, but the thinning of her lips and slight fluttering of her wings suggested she didn't quite appreciate my forgetfulness. Not even a little bit. I quickly reminded her about her keeping my parents' deaths a complete secret to even things up.

"I can't believe one of our employees did this." She ran her finger over the wrapping on my head. "Why?"

"What do you mean, why?" I laughed. "They wanted me dead. I thought that much was apparent from the extra hole in my head."

She rolled her eyes. "It's not a hole. It's more of a gouge."

"Gouge, huh?" I fingered the wound again, unable to feel anything through the heavy wrappings. "Bet it makes me look extramanly."

She chuckled. "Not really. In fact, it makes you look like you just got a haircut from a blind mouse." I winced, but Izzy wasn't finished, "You really are lucky to be alive. If Clark hadn't heard the shot and raced down the hall, who knows what might've happened?"

Fucking Clark. The damn guy was underfoot every time I turned around. Now I owed him my life, when what I really wanted was to take his when I pictured Izzy's mouth pressed to his. "I would've taken care of it," I said.

Neither of us believed a word of that.

"Did he see anyone?" I asked.

She shook her head. "He saw a shadowy figure escaping down the hallway but couldn't give the cops a good description." She paused, her wings fluttering slightly. "He was much too worried about you."

Great. I now felt even worse for wishing an STD on the guy.

"What were you doing at your office anyway?" Izzy asked when silence filled the curtained room. "You never stay later than the first ten minutes of happy hour."

I laughed at her joke, which sent a wave of pain through my brain. I quickly quieted. "I was trying to learn more about my mother's death and dear old dad's subsequent prison stay. I thought . . . if I found out more . . . I might find out the who."

"The who?"

I nodded, instantly regretting it. "Yeah. The who. As in who cares about a murder thirty years ago?"

She frowned, rubbing her arms with her hands as if warding off a chill. "You can't still think this is about your parents."

"What else could it be about?" Sure, I'd ruffled a few feathers of the winged and nonwinged variety, but most of those wings were either soothed by the former Tooth Fairy or now walked with a limp. This had to be about what had happened thirty years ago.

Had to be.

Because if it wasn't about that, bullet to the head aside, we were in very serious danger.

CHAPTER 57

I walked out of the hospital a few hours later, wearing a pilfered hospital gown and slippers after Izzy refused to aid my escape by getting me clean clothes. Of course, the doctors had argued over my impending departure as well, but the bleeding had stopped and the bullet hadn't hit anything vital. According to Izzy it would've had to travel pretty deep to hit my pea-sized brain.

Ignoring her and the doctors, I shuffled out of the hospital, a large swath of blue hair missing from the top of my head. I wasn't concerned, though. Not until I caught my reflection in the window of a passing taxi. I looked like death. Blood had stained my skin, turning my pale face the same color as a tomato.

That explained why not a single taxi pulled to the curb in response to my whistle. Izzy walked up behind me, and a few seconds later, a cab tore across two lanes of traffic to stop in front of her. The driver barely paid me a single glance. Izzy helped me inside, much to my dismay, and we set off for my apartment.

The cab hit a few bumps along the way, causing me to wince in pain. Izzy, true to her winged evilness, patted my arm and said, "Suck it up."

To which I replied with a manly whimper.

When the cab pulled to the curb in front of my apartment building, I slowly got out, my head now pounding. I longed for an extra-large glass of whiskey and hours of uninterrupted sleep. Neither of which I would be getting this dark night.

Not if Izzy had anything to do with it.

She insisted, once we made the torturous climb up the stairs, on keeping the whiskey from me as well as denying me much-needed sleep. "The doctor said I need to wake you up every few hours," she said, helping me into my bed. Once I was settled, she tucked a blanket around me and then sat on the edge of the bed next to me. Silence filled the room, as did a slight chill. "I'm scared, Blue," she finally whispered.

I shared her fear, but for a far different reason. A part of me, a stupid, foolish part, wanted to pull her into my arms, to take away the fear, but I couldn't. I would only end up hurting her. Like my father had my own mother. Instead I feigned sleep, letting out a snore. Without another word, she slowly stood and left the bedroom, the glow of the moonlight reflecting off her wings and illuminating the room.

Once she disappeared behind my bedroom curtain-door I sat up, running a finger through the swath of missing hair on top of my head. I really was lucky to be alive. I smiled into the darkness. Someone was getting nervous. And that was good. Nervous people made mistakes. And mistakes made it a hell of a lot easier to catch them.

Then it would be over.

And I would leave.

Forever.

After I ditched Right and Left, again, I headed to the oldest and wealthiest part of town. A place too good for streets of gold; instead they were paved with platinum. This was the sort of place a man like me would never fit in. Not that I cared one way or another. I wasn't here for myself. I was here for Izzy. I sucked in a lungful of cigarette smoke as I gathered my courage. A woman in a black-sheep coat strolled passed, her upper lip rising with disgust. I tipped my invisible cap, showing off the swath of missing blue hair. The woman gasped and hurried away.

Smiling, I threw my cigarette down, crushing it under the heel of my expensive loafers. I double-checked the snub-nosed .38 in the holster on my side. Better safe than sorry about last night's attempted murder. My head still pounding as a vivid reminder of my near-death experience, I headed for the ornate door of the fancy mansion in the heart of the city. My mind was focused on the mission at hand.

A mission I was fairly sure would end badly.

But it had to be done. I owed Izzy as much.

CHAPTER 58

I knocked on the door of the hundred-year-old mansion with apprehension. I shouldn't be here, I thought again. But it was too late. A maid in a black dress and white apron, like you see in the old movies, opened the door. "Yes?" she asked politely.

"Um . . . hi . . . I'm here to see Mr. Boyer."

A wrinkle grew on her forehead. "Mr. Boyer isn't accepting visitors at the moment."

"Of course," I said, remembering an article I'd read a few months ago about Clark's grandfather, the patriarch and CEO of Boyer Industries, who was, by all reports, gravely ill. According to the reporter, there was no clear front-runner for his replacement. I wondered if Clark wanted the job. He seemed like a perfect choice, born and bred to take over the family business. I approved wholeheartedly, mostly so his ass would be out of my blue hair. Then I remembered that I wouldn't be around after I closed this case. Izzy would need a partner.

Damn it.

I cleared my throat. "I'm here to see the youngest Mr. Boyer. Clark." Doreen, the bitchy receptionist, had told me Clark would be here. I hoped she wasn't wrong. I looked forward to searching the city for him nearly as much as I did having to offer up my thanks for his saving my life and then handing my business and my fairy over to him.

The confusion cleared and she gave me a soft smile. "Yes, of course. Please come in while I tell Mr. Clark that you're here."

I thanked her, wiped my feet on the doormat, which looked to be plated in gold-leaf lettering—the real stuff—and stepped inside a piece of New Never City history. The Boyer House stood on prime New Never City real estate, with more than twelve bedrooms, the same number of full baths, and enough art and other expensive knick-knacks to tempt the most honest of citizens.

One could only imagine how my fingers itched to case the place.

"If you'll wait in the library," the maid said, motioning toward a room the size of the entire floor of Reynolds & Davis. It was filled with books bound in Kobe leather and embossed in gold. Books no one in his right mind would dare open, let alone read, for fear of devaluing them. "Mr. Clark will be with you momentarily," she said, closing the library door behind me.

I swallowed the temptation to shove a few first editions into my jacket as my gaze scanned the wealth and privilege Clark had grown up around. I knew Izzy came from a similar, albeit smaller and winged, background. I wondered if they talked about their wealthy pasts. Told stories about the desperate times they'd had to use a silver rather than a platinum spoon. I shook my head, ridding it of such hateful thoughts.

Clark had no more choice in his lineage than I did in my own or Izzy did in the color of her wings. I needed to stop feeling jealous and thank him for saving me. I owed him that much. Hell, I owed the guy my life.

The library door creaked open. I turned toward the sound, expecting to see Clark standing in the entry. But it wasn't him. It was another man, an older man with slightly stooped shoulders and wrinkles lining his weathered face. Only a few wisps of blue-grey hair covered his balding head. This had to be Clark's grandfather.

His yellowed eyes slowly focused on me. "No. It can't be."

My head swiveled to the left and then the right. "Sir?"

"My God." He staggered toward me, his full weight on the cane in his shaking hand. "My son," he said. "You've come home. I knew you would."

Son? What the hell? "I think there's been some sort of mistake," I began, only to be interrupted when the library door opened for a second time. This time the man in the doorway froze, his eyes bouncing from me to the older man and back again.

Clark looked terrified, his eyes wide and a sheen of sweat covering his forehead. "Grandfather," he said in a high pitch to the older man as he pushed inside the library. "It's time for your medication."

My eyes stayed locked on the confused older gentleman as Clark led him from the library. When he disappeared around the corner with a young, very hot nurse, Clark returned to the library, a tight smile on his lips. "You shouldn't be here, Blue. My grandfather isn't well."

Guilt filled me. "Sorry about that . . . Doreen told me you'd be here, and I wanted to clear the air sooner rather than later."

"Clear the air?" he repeated. "How so?"

I took a few steps toward the large marble fireplace. Thanking him for saving my life would be easier if I didn't have to look at his perfectly straight teeth and overly waxed eyebrows. "About last night. The shooting . . ."

"I thought that might be why you're here."

"Yeah, well . . ." I stalled, unable to get the word "thanks" out of my mouth. "I just wanted to . . ." As the words left my lips, a bead of sweat slid down Clark's forehead. I frowned at the dark-colored per-spiration. My mind searched for a variety of diseases and other rea-sons for the odd color. I paused, studying his face.

"You were saying?" he prompted.

I blinked a few times. A missing piece of the puzzle, the one I'd been trying to solve for the last thirty years, slipped into place as the bead ran down his cheek. "Oh, shit," I got out before a very heavy and expensive vase slammed into the back of my skull.

CHAPTER 59

"You should've let me kill him last night," a woman's voice screeched. I struggled to focus on the speaker, but my eyes refused to cooperate. "Now he's bleeding all over the carpet . . ."

Clark's voice drifted from somewhere overhead. "I never thought he'd figure it out. But when I saw him in the library, I knew he knew."

Sadly I didn't know shit. Other than Clark and his lady friend had bashed my head in. Oh, and that Clark and I shared similar DNA. Cousins, I guessed, as I lay gazing up at the portrait above the fireplace. A portrait of the original Boyer clan. Two blue-haired brothers—my father, for whom I was a dead ringer, and his brother, who could have been Clark's twin—sat next to their smiling wives.

Add in the fact that Grandfather Boyer had thought I was his son.

A long-lost son.

A blue-haired one.

The very same color Clark was trying desperately to hide from the world. I knew from personal experience what black shoe polish looked like when applied to cover up blue hair.

The pieces fell into place. I'd been so stupid. All along Clark had been right there. PI rule number one: The most obvious answer was usually the right one. Or was it something about getting drunk and naked with an ogre was bound to turn out poorly? Either way, the truth had been staring me in the face for weeks. Or rather had been in the office down the hall.

Somehow Clark had arranged for James to join Reynolds & Davis; then he himself had come aboard. When James failed to kill me, Clark had turned to arson to keep his family secrets. I shook my head, causing it to ache even more.

That wasn't right.

Two things bothered me about the scenario. First, Clark had an air-tight alibi for the night that Izzy's brownstone burned to the ground. Me. I'd carried his drunken ass home. Unless he had wings, and big ones at that, he couldn't have made it across town in time to torch the brownstone. And second, why would Clark care enough to hide something that happened almost thirty years ago?

I was missing something. Something important. But for the life of me, literally, I couldn't figure out what it was. I let out a small groan as the pounding in my brain intensified.

"Welcome back," the feminine voice whispered. "I was worried I'd hit you a little too hard."

My gaze started to focus on the blonde standing over me, broken shards of vase in her manicured hands. "Doreen," I said through clenched teeth. Hell, I should've known she was in on it from day one. She'd been hired first, a few weeks before James. And more to the point, she had never quite appreciated my wit or electrical charm.

I wiped the back of my head, and my hand came away bright red with blood. Not a great sign. I glanced at Doreen and frowned. "Can't say I'm real happy to see you."

She let out a calculated laugh. "Clark worried you knew the truth. But I told him he was wrong. You don't know anything."

Given my current predicament, she wasn't far off. Not that I'd admit it. I'd die first, which, seeing the cold look in her eyes, was much more than a slight possibility. I decided to go on the offensive, attacking the weakest link—Clark. "Attempting to kill your own cousin, your own flesh and blood," I said to him. "That's gotta be worth a few eons in hell."

He frowned. "I told you he knew he was a Boyer."

"Clark," Doreen said. "Don't be a fool. He's fishing."

I laughed, slowly staggering to my feet. Doreen reached into her jacket, pulling out a snub-nosed .38. I patted my own pocket. My snub-nosed .38. Son of a bitch. "You plan to shoot me with my own gun? What kind of person does that?"

"A smart one," she sneered. "Everyone knows how depressed you've been since your darling Isabella started dating Clark ... Add in your heavy drinking, and no one will be that surprised ..."

"Faking a suicide? Really?" I stifled a yawn. "Whose brilliant idea is that?" Clark flinched, and my eyes narrowed on his face. I took a leap of faith. "Ah, dear cousin, can't say I'm surprised. No imagination."

His lips thinned. "I have plenty of imagination. I planned all of this, and you never suspected a thing."

Bastard had a point. "Why?" I asked. "What do you care if Boyer blood runs in my veins? It's not like I'm the next in line for the Boyer fortune." Even as I said it, I knew I'd made a grave mistake. I was the heir. The prodigal cousin Clark had talked about. That was why he wanted me out of the picture, to keep the fortune for himself. A part of me felt relieved. Greed I understood. It made people do things they normally wouldn't.

Clark grabbed the gun from Doreen and took aim at my chest. "I didn't want it to come to this. But I have no choice." His finger tightened on the trigger. "Now, tell me, how much does Isabella know?"

"So you can decide whether or not to kill her?" I shook my head. "Well, forget it. She has no idea about you." Which I suspected was less than true. I thought back to the night at Izzy's brownstone, listening in on her and Clark's "date." At the time I'd thought she was merely interested in Clark, but now I wondered if there wasn't more to it. She'd asked him question after question about his childhood. About the Boyer clan.

Had Izzy suspected I was a Boyer all along? Was that why she'd hired Clark in the first place? As the pieces slid into place, my anger ignited, sending a jolt of electricity through me. How dare she lie to me. Again.

"You better not be lying," he said, waving the gun in my direction. "I'd hate to have to hurt one feather on Isabella."

The rage burning inside me at Izzy's betrayal shifted to another target. One with similar DNA. "Don't even think about touching her," I warned.

"Kind of hard not to touch the woman I'm going to spend the rest of my life with." He paused, finger tensing on the trigger. "So sorry you won't be around for the wedding . . . or the wedding night."

CHAPTER 60

"Izzy will never marry you," I yelled as Clark started to squeeze the trigger. His finger stilled, much to my delight. Not that I had a follow-up to my statement. Hell, for all I knew, she would be the next Mrs. Boyer. The very thought sent another bolt of electricity through me.

"Shoot him already," Doreen said. "He's stalling."

"Am not," I lied, trying to think of a way to do just that. Keeping Clark talking seemed like my best bet, so I went with it. "I'm just curious as to how Clark put this all together. Murdering me before I could learn the truth behind my birth in order to keep the Boyer money all to himself wasn't a bad plan at all."

"You think this is about the money?" He laughed and lowered the gun.

"It's not?" Then why had he tried to kill me? Hell, we didn't know each other that well. Usually it took a few weeks before someone wanted me dead. Okay, a few days. But those were strictly business days.

He shook his head. "Do you know what it's like to live in the shadow of someone else?"

From the way he was looking at me, I guessed he wanted my sympathy. Sort of hard to feel with a gun aimed at your nuts, but I gave it a valiant effort. An effort that fell short when I let out a small scoff. The gun in Clark's hand rose back to my chest. I swallowed another snort of disdain, motioning for him to continue. "Go on with your whining," I said, unable to stop myself.

The gun steadied in his hand.

I closed my eyes, blowing out a harsh breath. "Please."

My plea had the desired effect, for the gun lowered a few inches. "All my life I'd heard stories about my long-lost cousin. The blue-haired boy who would be king." His gaze rolled over me, burning with hate. "Until a few months ago I thought you were dead like your mother and father. Then I saw a newspaper article on this up-and-coming PI blessed with the very power I'd spent my life longing for. And I knew—"

"Blessed?" I let out a bark of bitter laughter. "You're kidding, right? This"—I rubbed my fingers together, generating sparks—"is not a blessing. It's a curse."

He shook his head sadly. "Only a few Boyer men have had the power. No one knows when or why they get it. But when they do get it, all too often they squander it like you have. Keeping it under lock and key rather than taking their rightful place among the gods." He paused to lick his lips. I could see the excitement building in his gaze as he talked about my curse like it was some sort of gift. Hell, if I could, I would have traded places with him. The Boyer curse had destroyed so many lives. But to Clark the price exceeded the cost.

"Your father failed to live up to his potential too, and it also cost him his life," he said, when I didn't comment on his god complex.

"Like father, like son. Is that it?" I took a step toward Clark, daring him to fire. "I squandered my power, as you call it, so I should die like my father before me?"

His lips twisted with humor. "More than you know, for both of us."

I tilted my head to the side. "Are you saying my father was murdered by yours?" How was that possible? From all accounts, my father had hanged himself in his prison cell, unable to live with the horrific murder of his beloved wife at his electrified hands.

Clark shrugged. "Not in the physical sense, though my father, God rest his soul, would've liked nothing more. But your dear old daddy took the chance away when he wrapped his bed sheet around his throat, dying alone in his cell five years to the day after your mother died."

I pictured a similar fate. Not death by my own hands, but dying alone, lying in a pool of blood as my final breath leaked out of my lungs. I didn't want to die. And I sure as hell didn't want to die today, at the hands of my own kin.

"My father hated his brother for never understanding the true power he possessed." The gun wavered in Clark's hand as he continued his tale. "Like you, he considered the power a curse, especially after your mother's death." His eyes took on a faraway glow. "If it helps, it was an accident. Your mother's death, I mean. He never meant to kill her."

I bit my lip, drawing blood.

Clark waved a hand toward the fireplace, the same place I'd stood moments before Doreen had tried to bash my head in. "She died right there. No one even heard her cries. The maid found her the next morning, but you and your father were already gone. No one knew what happened to you. They captured your father a few hours later, but you weren't with him. We believed you were dead, killed by your father's hands, until a few months ago, when I saw the article about you after you solved the missing-jeweled-mittens case. I guess your father left you on the steps of the orphanage before his capture."

I frowned. If what Clark said was true, why had my father bothered to leave me anywhere? Traveling with a screaming infant was hard enough. Why add the complication of a kid after you'd just murdered your wife and a hundred cops were on your tail? Unless he'd feared what would happen if he didn't take me with him.

Clark let out a loud sigh. "If only you would have forgotten about your past, none of this would be necessary. But from the moment I first met you, I knew you would never let it go. Which left me with one choice."

"Kill me outright before dear old granddad found out the truth?" I shook my head. "But not before you tied up one last loose end." A cold smile grew on Clark's face and I knew I'd guessed right. He hadn't saved me from Doreen's bullet last night due to some misplaced sense of family loyalty. Instead, he'd stopped her from killing me in order to find out how much Izzy knew. Clark wasn't as dumb as I'd first thought. He knew killing me would bring down my partner's wrath.

"Isabella can live or die." He paused, eyes intent on mine. An electrical current beyond any I'd ever felt grew inside me. Burning hotter and deeper until I thought I would explode. But Clark wasn't finished. "The choice is yours."

CHAPTER 61

"Not quite," Izzy's voice called from the doorway of the library. All three of us spun to face her and the nine-millimeter in her hand. "Drop the weapon," she said to Clark, who did as she ordered, laying his gun on the floor at his feet.

He held up his hands. "Now, Isabella, this isn't what it looks like."

"Really?" she said tilting her head to one side. "It looks like you and Doreen cooked up a plot to kill Blue before he found out he was the true Boyer heir."

The words "like father, like son" flitted through my mind again. And suddenly all the pieces fell into place. Hiding my being the Boyer heir was only part of his reason for murdering me. I swallowed back a flash of electrical rage. "That's not the only reason Clark wants me dead."

"Oh?" Izzy asked, the gun steady in her slender hands.

I took a menacing step toward Clark, blue sparks raining from my fingers like wildfire. He shrank back. "Want to fill Izzy in?" I growled. "Tell her how badly you wanted to cover up a murder from thirty years ago?"

"I did it for us," he said. "All of us. The Boyer name is all we have."

"Bullshit," I said, our bodies only a foot apart. One touch and his murderous ass would be toast. Literally. "You did it for you. You hired James to kill me; then you burned up my office and had Doreen torch Izzy's brownstone, not to mention murdering an elderly nurse to keep everyone from finding out that it was your father who murdered my mother. Not mine. And then he framed his own brother for the gruesome act."

Clark had the grace to blush. Not a great look on any man, but even less appealing on a pale one with black shoe polish in his hair. Another zap of current flickered through me. The bottoms of my boots started to smoke. I took a step toward him, the desire to choke the life out of him nearly overwhelming. But I resisted. Killing Clark wouldn't bring my parents back. Besides, for better or worse—and I firmly suspected more of the latter—Clark was one of my few living relatives.

"My father knew the truth, knew that it was his own brother who'd killed my mother," I said. "That's why he hid me away. He knew that if he didn't, one day I'd meet with an unfortunate incident too. Just like my mother. He didn't hang himself, dying alone in a cell because of guilt at taking the life of the one woman he ever loved. He did it because he couldn't stand living without her."

Izzy's gaze flew to my face.

But it was too late for me. For us. The burning inside me grew too great. She waved Doreen and Clark to the right, away from me. "Blue," she called. "Are you all right?"

"I've had better days," I choked out as the current rocketed through me in waves of fire. I was losing control. My body shook as the buzz of electricity reached epic proportions. "Get the hell out of here. Now," I warned as blue light exploded from my fingers. For a moment, my entire body went numb. I couldn't see. I couldn't hear. Everything was frozen.

Then the blue light dissipated, leaving the scene unfolding in front of me.

A sight I'd feared for the last year.

Izzy was lying on the ground, as still as death.

Her eyes were fixed and dilated.

CHAPTER 62

I dropped down next to Izzy, careful not to touch her for fear I'd cause her more injury, the rest of the world around us forgotten. Nothing mattered except for the woman on the floor. "Come on," I said, voice thick. "You can't die on me."

Sirens screamed in the distance.

But they were too late.

Izzy was gone.

I'd destroyed her.

A tear leaked from the corner of my eye. It rolled down my cheek and onto Izzy's soft skin. I lifted my finger, brushing it away.

By some miracle, at my touch, her chest jumped and she let out a loud gasp. "Izzy," I said, pulling her into my arms. "You're alive."

She pushed at my chest with her hands. "Not for long if you keep smothering me."

"Oh." I let her go. She stayed sitting up, wavering only a little. "Are you all right?" I asked.

"I've had better days," she repeated my words back at me. Then she glanced around the now empty room. "You let them get away?"

My eyes followed hers. I shrugged. "I had a more pressing matter to attend to."

"Damn it, Blue," she began.

I cut her off. "I'm so sorry, Izzy. I never wanted to hurt you."

"Stop it," she said. "None of this was your fault. I should've—"

Two paramedics and a handful of cops entered the room, putting an end to our conversation. I watched as they checked Izzy's vitals, jabbed a needle into her arm, and loaded her on a gurney. Much to her dismay. But I wouldn't let her argue. She'd nearly died today. A trip to the hospital to get checked out seemed like the next logical

204 • *J.A. Kazimer*

step. Or so I told her when she tried to leap off the gurney. Thankfully the paramedics were prepared, shooting a few milligrams of sedative into her IV. As her eyes grew hazy, she reached for my arm, but I pulled away in time. "Blue," she whispered.

I leaned down to hear her. "I'm right here."

"You better be," she said. Her head lolled to the side, and she closed her eyes.

Detective Locks arrived a few minutes later as Izzy was wheeled past. I started to follow them out the door, but Locks stopped me. "Care to tell me what happened here?" she asked.

I shook my head.

"Funny thing," she said. "I found Clark Boyer outside, unconscious, along with an unknown woman. Both had been tased."

"Is that so?" Had my power surge knocked him out as he and Doreen attempted to escape? I smiled at the thought. It served him right. I vowed to have a nice chat with my cousin real soon, and it would end with more than a little jolt of electricity. But now wasn't the time. Clark and Doreen would pay for their sins. By the time I was done with him, Clark would understand the difference between a gift and a curse.

I'd make sure of it.

CHAPTER 63

A month after the debacle at the Boyer mansion I settled back against the silken sheets of the Hushed Little Baby Hotel in the heart of Wonderland. I'd spent the last week at the hotel, weighing my options. None of which sounded good at the moment. I wasn't ready to go back to work as a PI just yet, nor was I interested in anything to do with the name Boyer, even though the Boyer family lawyers wouldn't leave me alone.

The last month of court hearings and accusations screamed by reporter after reporter faded as I stretched out on the bed, willing my mind to forget my cousin's face as the jury foreman read his sentence—life without the possibility of parole. And not life at some fancy Club Fey prison either. Hard time. In a prison even smaller than the one my father had resided in during the last five years of his life.

Even as the foreman read the verdict and I watched a sobbing Clark being led away in handcuffs, I knew it wasn't over. It wouldn't be until I made good on my promise to leave New Never City and my partner. I couldn't take the chance of hurting her again.

Izzy didn't quite see it that way, though. "How can you leave? We still have open cases. What about the missing fairies? You promised Peyton that you'd find them," she yelled as we sat in her office after I'd told her of my decision to move far, far away. "I don't understand. Please, Blue . . . don't do this."

Though I knew she was right, that I was walking away before I found the missing fairies for Peyton, I tried to explain why I had to leave, to put words to what I felt, how I'd felt when I held her lifeless body in my arms, but they wouldn't come. So I said, instead of answering her, "I'll e-mail you an address where you can send my things." And then I walked out the doors of what was now Davis Securities.

My heart burned in my chest.

I'd done the right thing.

I knew it, even if Izzy didn't.

I took a drink from my half-empty glass of expensive whiskey, enjoying as it burned a path down my throat and into my stomach. Pain was good. It meant I was still alive. Still feeling, even if the rest of me felt nothing. On the TV news ticker at the bottom of the screen, updates from the Tooth Fairy election scrolled across the television. Clayton had won by a few hundred votes. I shook my head, wondering if those few hundred votes matched the names of the few hundred missing fairies. I wouldn't put it past the twins.

A knock at the hotel room door drew me from my dark musings. I put the whiskey glass on the night table and slowly got out of bed. "Yeah?" I called.

"Room service," a muffled voice responded.

I opened the door. "I didn't order—" The sight in front of me so surprised me that words failed to form on my tongue. "Izzy?" I choked out. "What the hell are you doing here?"

"Can I come in?" she asked, rather than answer my pointed question.

I motioned her inside, still unable to process the fact that she was here. In my hotel room. And from the look of her tanned legs poking out from a trench coat covering her from shoulder to midthigh, she was nearly or completely naked underneath.

Izzy stepped inside, her gaze taking in the almost empty bottle of whiskey, the rumpled bedcovers, and my bare chest. "We damn well better be alone, Blue."

I grinned. "We are."

"Good." She gripped the belt around her waist. "We have a few things to discuss."

"Is that so?"

"Yes."

I tore my gaze from her legs. "How did you find me?"

She grinned. "I learned how to track people from the best investigator."

"Why are you here?" I asked, my voice hoarse with equal parts lust and fear. Lust won out as she slowly untied the belt holding her trench coat closed. "Izzy, I don't think . . ."

"Then don't think, Blue. Forget everything but right now. This moment." Her coat pooled at her feet, leaving a very naked, very lovely half human, half fairy in front of me. Every thought I had flew from my mind, and all I could think to do was take her into my arms.

Which was exactly what I did.

Neither of us speaking as sparks exploded around us.

The jarring buzz of Izzy's cell phone woke me in the middle of the night. I reached for the ringing phone on the nightstand, careful not to disturb the fairy lying next to me, our bodies close but not touching. She slept the sleep of angels—or more to the point, of a woman who'd experienced multiple, electrifying orgasms. My hand fumbled along the edge of the nightstand until my fingers curled around the phone. I answered with a growl. "What?"

"Is that you, Blue?" The phone crackled with static. ". . . Izzy . . . there?"

"Yeah, it's Blue," I said. "Izzy's asleep. What do you want?"

The phone cut in and out, and for a second I thought I'd lost him. "Peyton? You still there?"

". . . missing . . . looked everywhere . . . help . . ."

"Can you repeat that?" I gripped the phone tighter. "You're breaking up."

A second later his voice burst from the phone. "Clayton's missing. I've looked everywhere, but no one has seen him. It's like he vanished into thin air like all those other fairies." He paused, voice thick with tears. "Please, Blue, you have to find my brother."

Don't miss Blue's first mystery, *The Fairyland Murders*, and J.A. Kazimer's F***ed-Up Fairytales series: *Curses!* and *Froggy Style*.

THE FAIRYLAND MURDERS
A Deadly Ever After Mystery
Not all endings are happy . . .

Blue Reynolds knows the darker side of New Never City—the side that's hopped-up on fairy dust and doesn't care if your house gets blown down. Rent's due and his PI business is all but make-believe. But even Blue shudders at having to chase after Isabella Davis, a freckle-nosed redhead five feet tall on her tiptoes . . . if you don't count the pretty pink wings.

Izzy is tough, and sneaky, and not too thrilled with the idea of being the new Tooth Fairy. The last six have been most gruesomely extracted. But Blue has a feeling that whoever is killing the Tooth Fairies is worse than your standard big bad psycho. The Fairy Council is hiding something. The Shadows are moving out into the light. And Blue is saddled with a shocking power that could take out half of New Never City . . .

J.A. KAZIMER

Not all endings are happy...

THE *Fairyland* MURDERS

CURSES!

I'm no hero. In fact, up until a couple of days ago, I was the villain. Kidnapped maidens, scared kids, stole magic tchotchkes—until I got into a little scrape with the union. Now I'm cursed with the worst fate in New Never City—no matter what I do, I gotta be nice.

So when a head-case princess named Asia barges into my apartment and asks me to find out who whacked her stepsister, Cinderella, I have no choice but to help her. And I'm more than willing to head back to her parents' castle and do some investigating if it means I can get into her black leather catsuit. Except this twisted sister has a family nutty enough to send the biggest baddest wolf running for the hills—and a freaky little curse of her own . . .

"More than f***ed-up. Demented. Hilarious."
—Mario Acevedo, author of *Werewolf Smackdown*

"Forget everything you know about Cinderella. J.A. Kazimer sets the record straight with humor and a hell of an imagination!"
—Jeanne C. Stein, national bestselling author

"A thoroughly fun read."
—Nicole Peeler, author of the Jane True series

CURSES!

A F***ed-Up Fairy Tale

J.A. KAZIMER

FROGGY STYLE

It ain't easy being green . . .
Jean-Michel La Grenouille has a lot going for him. He's a prince.
Handsome. Filthy rich. And definitely charming. But he also spent
his first few years as a fly-catching, pond-dwelling frog. All that
saved him was the kiss of the One, the girl who saw nobility through
his slimy form and fell into True Love. Okay, fine. Technically she
was a toddler who tried to eat him, but whatever. The curse broke,
and as long as he finds and marries her by his thirtieth birthday, he's
a free man.

Trouble is, he's going to be thirty in ten days, and he's getting some
seriously cold-blooded feet. He's pretty sure Princess Sleeping
Beauty is the One. But his best man has some villain issues, his
in-laws-to-be belong in a really *special* castle, and a smoking-hot
lady biker named Lollie Bliss has him rethinking all this
happily-ever-after stuff. Oh, and he may have accidentally put
out a hit on his blushing bride. Oopsie.

Froggy Style

It ain't easy being green...

A F***ed-Up Fairy Tale

J.A. KAZIMER

About the Author

Originally from Cleveland, Ohio, **J.A. Kazimer** escaped at a young age and now lives and writes in Denver, Colorado. Kazimer holds a master's degree in forensic psychology and has worked as a PI and a bartender.

For current works and more information, visit www.jakazimer.com, read *The New Never News* fairytale blog at http://thenewnevernews.blogspot.com, or follow on Twitter @jakazimer.